BACKROAD BLUES

HEIDI KLOSE

Cover illustration by Anastasia Salikhova

Seagull Publications, Niagara Falls, Ontario
ISBN: 978-1-988031-22-4

BACKROAD BLUES

DEDICATED

to my daughter Marnie who inspired me
to write this book.

In 1995, she and her friend Stasia, went on a road adventure after they had both completed their schooling. From Niagara, Canada they drove south to Key West, back up the Florida Peninsula, across to San Diego, passing through New Orleans. From California they drove diagonally through the U.S. back to Ontario. They did all this in a beat-up VW Westfalia camper. Some of their never-ending troublesome experiences, a lot with AAA, are mentioned in the chapter 'Meghan and Sarah's Blues.'

In this book I have woven two legends about a pact with the devil together. One of these is in Goethe's Faust, the titular character of which is, in my story, Jonathan. My character desperately seeks knowledge from the Prince of Darkness to find those responsible for the murder of his beloved young bride Margie in a graveyard twenty-some years ago. The other legend is that of Robert Johnson who, at the Crossroads in Clarksdale, Mississippi, sold his soul to the devil so that he could be the best blues guitarist in the world.

I wanted to experience the Blues Highway with my husband this year, hear the music, enjoy southern cooking, and see the beautiful architecture, especially in the French Quarter of New Orleans. Sadly, the Covid-19 outbreak put an end to this. At this point in time, we cannot cross the border into the United States. Perhaps we will be able to in the near future.

I have been in Nashville, home of country music, Memphis, the birthplace of rock'n'roll and home of the blues, and New Orleans, which gave the gift of jazz to the world. They are truly unique cities with so much history, so much inspiring, uplifting music to offer. The world is also a better place because of the amazing music that was born in the Mississippi Delta—blues, jazz, soul as well as Dixieland and gospel.

Music is there for you and me

Music—it will set you free

Heidi Klose

CONTENTS

CHAPTER I

THE PACT

DARKNESS. It's all around me. It's all encompassing. I breathe it in and exhale its odorless, poisonous gases. But it's not only occupying every space and crevice outside of my body, it's within me. It has morphed my heart into a black pumping station where cold, grimy liquids flow laboriously into arteries and veins, all trying to reject this toxic fluid from traversing.

This nothingness has taken my soul, if I still have one, and made that spot within me, wherever that may be, into a black hole, larger than any in our interstellar universe. There is no light at the end of the tunnel, no beacon to entice me to step forward toward a light, my way to everlasting happiness, contentment, euphoria. Those are all in the past, the distant past, so long ago that I only vaguely remember those precious moments of warmth, smiles, the smell of her hair, embracing, her sweet surrender. It was all stolen from me in one short moment, in the darkness of a gloomy, disturbing place on a night grim and sullen, a night when loathsome, barbarous recreants betrayed her trust and in the process darkened my soul and made me into this.

Oh, I know that they talk about me in the village where I go when my monthly disability check has been deposited into my account at the bank. I bicycle in from my cabin to pick up a few items, some groceries and other essentials.

"Hi Jonathan," little Billy will shout. He is young,

innocent and too naïve to realize that I am a long-haired, malodorous latter-day hippie who lives like a hermit in a cabin willed to me by my late uncle. "Beautiful day, isn't it?" he continues. "I'm gonna go fishing with my dad after school today. Will I see you by the lake?"

I smile and nod at Billy. "Maybe. You will if I'm not too busy," I tell him. Busy at what? I don't do anything, Well, not very much.

"Good morning, Jonathan," says the teller behind the counter in the bank very sternly. "How much are you withdrawing today?"

I tell her, take my money and head over to the grocery store. I know I'm being watched, especially if I go to the hardware store. One of those sets of prying eyes sent the RCMP to my cabin in the British Columbia wilderness a few months ago. Probably thought I was another Unabomber, living alone in a run-down cabin for over a decade, bicycling everywhere even though there is a large vehicle covered by a big tarp parked in the driveway. But, after a very thorough search, the police officers found nothing suspicious in my cabin or shed, no bomb-making material, kits, guns, rifles, threatening letters or lists of people I wanted to kill. There is no list, well, not written down, because I don't remember their names, but there is a list in my mind, of faces, evil, grotesque images of killers that I must eliminate.

Angels watch over the innocent. Do they really? Do they watch over little children? Because I've been in a children's ward of a cancer hospital where four-year-olds run around with bandages around their heads after malignant tumors have been removed from their brains. Children are killed every day, in war, in famine. Where are their angels?

On a coffee break? There were no angels watching over my beloved as there should have been. She was so beautiful, innocent, perfect.

God helps those who help themselves, well what good is he then? If you can help yourself then you don't need God. I can't help myself, so it looks like God won't help me. But I need help, need it desperately. If I am going to get out of this nocturnal nothingness I need someone to guide my way. I need a plan, a destination.

Think, Jonathan, think. How do people suddenly become someone they never were before, or achieve the unachievable? How can I turn this asinine, half-witted brain of mine into a master mind? How do I become a genius? How can I remember the long-forgotten?

***

Jonathan sat on an old lawn chair outside his cabin. His battery-powered transistor radio, placed on a small round table on his porch, hooked up with two metal coat hangers for reception, began to play blues music from a station south of the British Columbia border. He looked up into the sky but the miraculous answer he needed was not written in the stars, nor was a meteor streaming across the night sky with an answer trailing behind it. No, Jonathan suddenly had his very own idea.

"I must get to the Crossroads."

***

The car began to shake violently from side to side. The wind was howling and the windows of the police car were rattling.

A torrent of water was gushing down from the clouds.

"We have to stop," said Lee. "The windshield wipers can't handle that much water. I can't see where I'm driving."

"There's a little motel about a mile up the road," said his partner Roy. "We'll have to stop there."

"And if they're full?"

"I'll sleep on a bench in the coffee shop if I have to. I don't care. As long as we're both warm and safe."

Just then one of the officers noticed headlights behind them.

"Who the hell is on this road tonight? There is a driving ban in this county until the storm has passed."

Lee pushed on the brakes and stopped his vehicle. "Yeah, maybe this guy didn't switch his radio on. I'll go outside to flag him down."

"I'll come with you to hang onto you so you don't fly away."

"Thanks, I don't want to do a Mary Poppins."

With their two flashlights, the officers indicated to the driver of the vehicle to stop. The person did as requested. He rolled down his door window.

"Is there a problem, officers?" he shouted.

"We're at the tail end of a hurricane. The winds are gusting over one hundred miles an hour. You're not supposed to be on the road tonight, sir."

"Sorry officers. I didn't know."

"There's a little motel just up ahead on your right. Stop there for the night and continue in the morning. It should all be over by then," said Roy.

"Thank you, yes, I will."

"Did you see his eyes?" asked Lee. "Kind of crazy looking, if you ask me."

but we'll take a bathroom break halfway through. We'll be stopping for lunch but only for a quick bite before we're underway again. And make sure to leave room for tonight's dinner because we're going to be dining at an exceptional restaurant in Memphis.

"From there we'll head on down and stop at the Crossroads, the intersection of Highways 49 and 61. The famous place where Robert Johnson, as legend has it, sold his soul to the devil so that he could play his guitar like no other. Many people believe that Johnson was the father of the blues, and indeed, he was one of the first to make a recording which is still in existence after such a long time.

"Before we reach each destination, whether it be a recording studio, a bar, a museum, a home or any other place that has its origin in the blues, I will provide you with a little bit of history. If you have any questions you can shout it out and I can let everyone know the answer, or just come to my seat at the front of the bus and I'll be happy to enlighten you."

"We are about to be enlightened!" joked the balding man with the goatee.

"Well, it's about time," said a man with olive skin and dark brown hair, sitting across the aisle from him.

"I do have beverages on board, alcoholic and non. If you'd like a drink just let me know. I've got beer, soda and water bottles. I guess it's a little early for alcoholic beverages."

"It's got to be twelve o'clock somewhere in the world and since none of us, except Big Mike, are driving, I'll have a beer, if you don't mind," said a mustached man.

"A bit early, don't you think, even for you, Dylan?" said the frizzy blond woman wearing jeans, a jersey blouse and a light-weight dark jacket, sitting beside him.

"I don't mind at all," replied the tour guide. "Mike, would you like a pop?"

"Sure," replied the bus driver. "I'll have a Coke. Thanks."

"Folks, I'll be playing some blues music over the intercom to get you into the mood, but not too loud so that you can still have private conversations," said the tour guide.

***

"Oh, look at those four people at the very back of the bus," said the woman who had earlier reprimanded her husband about his drinking, to the woman sitting directly across the aisle.

"Yeah?" responded her friend, a smartly dressed brunette wearing a t-shirt, jeans and booties with a side zipper.

"They're Canadian."

"Really? And you know this how, Brooke?"

"Oh, you know, Sally, they all kind of look alike."

"They do? In what way?"

"They're different. You know, their skin, it's kind of white and pasty."

"You're kidding me, right?"

"No, no. Take a good look."

"And why is their skin white and pasty?"

"'Cause they live in the great white north. They don't get as much sunshine up there as we do."

"You're saying the sun doesn't shine in Canada?"

"Well, it does but it's not as strong. You feel that right away when you walk over the bridge from Niagara Falls over to the Canadian side."

"Really!"

"Yeah. The temperature dips right away and you get a real chill."

"I see."

"They're actually allergic to the sun, you know."

"Canadians!"

"Yup. You see that in Florida. Millions of Canadians drive or fly there each winter. Even though they're used to living like Emperor Penguins in the winter it gets to them after a while and then they escape south. That's why they call them snow birds."

"Penguins are at the South Pole. They don't come from the north."

"I know that. It's just an expression."

"How do they take the heat?"

"Not well."

"They're all allergic to sunlight. That's why they only come out of their motels in the evenings, otherwise they'd get sun rashes. And they put gobs of suntan lotion on, number 60, otherwise they burn to a crisp."

"Why do they bother going south?"

"'Cause even becoming nocturnal is better than living in a white hell all winter."

"Really? Wow! I didn't know that. And yeah, they do look kind of pale, almost sickly."

"We gotta let them cross the border more often so they can capture some rays, get some vitamin D."

"It's the only decent thing to do."

"Brooke, what are you babbling on about now?" asked her husband, Dylan.

"Very funny daaling. I was just mentioning to Sally that those four people at the very back of the bus are probably Canadians."

"Oh. So now, you're psychic?"

"Oh, shut up," replied his wife, quite annoyed. Turning to Sally, Brooke continued. "I think that tour guide sounds kind of Canadian as well."

"Really?" said Sally. "Because Californians all sound Canadian."

"Or Canadians sound like Californians," reasoned Brooke.

"That might be too."

***

After a two-hour drive, the bus stopped in the parking lot of a restaurant situated beside a large hotel at the intersection of two major highways. All the passengers disembarked and walked into a restaurant. Some lined up to use the restroom, others sat down at tables.

Dylan and Brooke, along with their friends Jordan and Sally, welcomed four others to their large table which had a seating capacity of eight.

"My name is Will," said a tall, broad shouldered man with dark brown hair graying at the temples. "Please let me make the introductions. This is my wife Meghan, her best friend Sarah and her husband Jim."

"Hi," said Meghan, who was a woman in her late forties, with hazel eyes, a welcoming smile, a few freckles on her cheeks, and long hair done up in a messy yoga bun. She was wearing black stretchy pants, a low-cut tie-dye cotton rainbow-colored t-shirt and bright yellow flip-flops.

"Hello," said Jim, a short, stocky, big-boned man with large hands.

"Pleased to meet you. I'm Dylan, this is my wife Brooke."

Pointing to his friends he said: "This is Jordan and his wife Sally."

"Pleasure's all ours," said Sarah, a fashionably dressed woman in her late forties, with horn-rimmed glasses, dressed in an a-line skirt, t-shirt and a blanket scarf which she removed and hung over the back of her chair.

A waitress brought the menus. Everyone at the table browsed through their list of options. The waitress returned in a very short time. Tourists on buses brought little time with them and they had to be served quickly.

"I think I'll have some taco tater tots," said Jim.

"Woah, big fella, that's pretty greasy and we're just sitting in the bus all day," said his wife Sarah. "Remember your blood work from a couple of weeks ago? Your cholesterol count is a bit high."

"I agree, we should eat something lighter. Justin said that we're going to have a big dinner tonight," added Meghan.

"Okay, okay. I'll just have a burger, no fries," Jim conceded, somewhat annoyed.

"How did you enjoy the Grand Ole Opry last night?" Dylan asked.

"Oh, it was grand all right. If you like country music, that is," replied Will.

"You're sayin' you don't?" asked Dylan.

"Today's country music is better than that twangy whining of years past, but no, it's not my favorite."

"You prefer the blues?"

"Depends. I always liked Prince and Eric Clapton, to my mind the two best guitarists this world has ever known. Eric has recorded and played a lot of blues songs. I remember watching a concert he did with B.B. King, and another with Stevie Ray Vaughan."

"Then why did you go on this trip?"

"Free tickets won by Meghan and Sarah. My wife wasn't going to give them up. I mean, who would? A trip from Nashville to New Orleans, with the accommodations and admission to the concert last night, all paid for."

"You got free tickets too? So did I, and so did my friend Jordan in an online contest. What a coincidence!"

"Yeah, is it ever! You know, country music is just the white man's version of the blues. Same story told over and over and over again, *ad nauseam*."

"You think?"

"Mhm. Let me give you an example." Will began to sing:

The old bitch, she left me
She left me alone
With four bratty children
With a mind of their own

"Too funny!"

"That's pretty much the story that's sung over and over again, isn't it?"

"Well, there are a few others, but you have a point, and talent too, I might add. You could sing that on *America's Got Talent*."

"Me? That's the last thing they need to improve their ratings."

"I didn't catch your name earlier," said Jordan, a man in his late forties who was showing the beginnings of a little paunch, to the person sitting beside him.

"Oh, it's Jim," said the muscular man.

"Like the other thirty-three passengers on this bus,

you're a blues fan, I imagine."

"Well, not exactly, although I don't mind a song or two now and then. I'm more of a stadium rock type of person. Bon Jovi, ah, Bryan Adams and such, a child of the nineties, I guess. How about you?"

"Aerosmith, Springsteen. My friend Dylan's a real blues fan. He's gone to see a lot of blues artists. We actually had a little garage band when we were in high school and he wanted to play the blues. But the rest of us wouldn't go for it. Teenagers were listening to Guns N' Roses back then and that's what we wanted to play. Anyways, we didn't really sound that great, and once Dylan left for college, that was the end for our little band of rock star wannabes."

"Oh, that's too bad."

"It's okay. Enough about me! What about you, Jim, what do you do for a living?" asked Jordan.

"I'm an electrician by trade. I own a business and have about a dozen guys working for me. And you, Jordan?"

"Hey! I'm a tradesman like you! Well, I started out that way, as an automotive mechanic. But I've got the good fortune of working for a really great company. I'm the manager of an automotive center now. Actually, my friend Dylan owns the car dealership. His father left it to him."

"Good for you, man. Any family?"

"Yup, two boys, twelve and eight." He took out his wallet and pulled out a picture.

"Nice-looking family you've got. Sarah and I have a boy and a girl."

"Million-dollar family."

"Wow, haven't heard that expression in a very long time. I think I once heard my grandfather say that."

"Don't know where that came from."

"Yeah. It's surprising what's in the back of one's mind."

***

After the tour guide had done his count to ensure no one had been left behind, he gave the thumbs up to the driver. The happy blues highway journey continued.

"Hey! Sarah!" Meghan shouted to her friend across the aisle looking out the window, listening to music on her iPhone. "Heard any good fishy music lately?"

Sarah turned her head, took out her earphone plugs and smiled. "Good guess. I'm listening to Phish."

"I still love them. You know this blues tour reminds me of our road trip way back when."

"It's been twenty-five years now. Can you believe it? Where has the time gone?"

"You've got that right. We were young, adventurous, perhaps a bit naïve."

"We were. Didn't really know exactly where we were going and put a lot of faith into that old VW camper of mine."

"Here we go again," mumbled Will.

"Oh gawd, do we have to listen to this one more time? We've heard your never-ending road trip a thousand times," said Jim.

"I'm surprised neither one of you wrote a book about it. Could have been a movie by now," added Will.

"You're just jealous that you didn't do anything that exciting in your twenties. You went to university, got a job and that was that," said Meghan.

"Meghan is right. All young people should take a year off after school and travel. It's good for them and you learn a lot more that you do in school or getting some low-level job right after graduating," said Sarah.

"Yes, yes, independence, get to know people, places and how to avoid people and get out of sticky situations."

"There's more..."

"Okay, so if you two want to reminisce, then sit together. Maybe the drone of the tires of this bus will drown you out," said Jim.

"Actually, I don't mind sitting beside you Jim, but I'm gonna listen to some music on my phone. No offense," said Will.

"None taken. I'll get mine out as well. I've got some U2, Aerosmith and Bon Jovi downloaded onto my device."

Jim stood up, got out of his seat and backed up a few feet in the aisle. Will did the same thing but took a few steps forward. Sarah moved over and sat beside Meghan.

"When was it exactly?" asked Sarah.

"Mid-October of 1995 and we came back in April of 1996, if I remember correctly?" replied Meghan.

"Sounds about right."

Chapter III

Meghan and Sarah's Blues

We're travelin' down the highway
The open road ahead
We thought it would be easy
Our nerves are shot instead
The camper keeps on stalling
At times gives up its ghost
It's triple A, it's towing trucks
That's what we see the most
That's why we're blue, oh yeah
We've got the backroad drivin' blues

Too young to be snowbirds, the million Canadian retirees who spend part of each winter in Florida, Meghan and Sarah decided to join this unique flock. Meghan, a light auburn-haired, brown-eyed twenty-something with pouty lips and an infectious smile, and Sarah, a green-eyed, dirty-blond young woman with a more serious demeanor, wearing secretary glasses, had attended the same high school in Niagara Falls. They were not the best of friends, but had met through friends of friends. They didn't have that much in common except for the fact that they both liked to travel. Meghan had traveled to Ireland to visit relatives in Killarney, and also to the continent where she had traveled with a cousin through Denmark, Norway and Sweden. Sarah had stuck to the North American continent and camped alone in the Maritimes, driving through New Brunswick, Nova Scotia and Prince Edward Island.

Meghan had just finished her Bachelor of Science and Sarah a college degree in Tourism. Both had kept in touch over the years and, once finished with their studies, decided they needed some time off before someone actually made them grow up, assume adult responsibilities and follow a path leading to a career. Sarah's beat-up camper, a Volkswagen Westfalia, slighted by being parked on a grassy incline behind the house, not even on the driveway, as the other cars owned by family members, was just waiting to go on a magical ride. And so it came to pass that the two young women decided to drive through America, well, not so much through, but drive the entire perimeter, first along the Atlantic coast to Key West in Florida, back up the peninsula and then west to Southern California, up the Pacific Coast and then across back east to, as Sarah liked to say, "Ontari-ari-ari-o, our home and native land."

"I'm feeling adventurous," said Sarah, as she looked over the road map of half a continent.

"I'm ready for some Fahrvergnügen," said Meghan.

"Some what?"

"Fahrvergnügen. Driving enjoyment. You as the owner of a Volkswagen should be familiar with that term."

"All right then, let's have some Farfargnoogen."

The two friends decided to hit the road. Well, they didn't really, but parts of their ready-for-the-junkyard Volkswagen Camper certainly did. Throughout their travels the camper would scrape against the pavement when it hit a pot hole and leave unidentifiable metallic thingamabobs strewn all around. At one point their muffler fell off and they had to tie it back on with some wire. Some bolts not fastened tightly enough loosened on a particularly bumpy road, and fell off, as did a tire which bounced happily into a ditch as witnessed by Sarah, in almost disbelief, in her rear view mirror. Meghan nonchalantly got out of the camper, which Sarah luckily had been able to keep on the paved portion of the road, and went back to retrieve the escapee. A call had to be made to AAA yet once again.

But it wasn't just the towing truck companies that came to their aid. In New Orleans the local police helped them. Sarah stood proudly beside an officer while Meghan took their picture. In Pasadena, the California Highway Patrol, or CHIPs, with which they were familiar from an old television series, came to their rescue. This time, Sarah would take Meghan's picture. Sarah's favorite photo of a rescue was herself putting gas into the gas tank of her Westfalia while standing on top of a large tow truck. They had run out of gas once again.

On a cold, overcast day, the two adventurers crossed into the United States by way of Niagara Falls and headed south towards their first destination, Washington D.C. After a few hours of traveling mainly on secondary roads, they decided to take a break. What they found was a coffee shop on the Cornell University campus. When they walked into the rickety diner, it was like stepping into the sixties. One of the hippies with long gray-streaked hair and sandals was playing his harmonica on an open stage. Sarah told Meghan that she had forgotten something in the camper. When she came back she had her friend's guitar in her hand. Sarah walked to the stage, sat on a wobbly chair and began playing Indigo Girls songs. Once she had finished, she was greeted with much applause. Sarah and

Meghan felt right at home in this communally open atmosphere. With their long hair and second-hand clothes, they felt almost at one with the hippies of years past. They enjoyed a cinnamon-flavored coffee and befriended some of the locals, but after a little while informed them that they had to go.

"Please come back next week," said one of the coffee shop patrons.

"Sure thing," replied Sarah as she winked at Meghan.

With very limited resources, their college and university having swallowed most of the earnings they had made in their summer jobs, they had to stretch the little money that they had. Most of their breakfasts were bought at truck stops and suppers would often be 99-cent breakfasts, a mere egg on toast with coffee. Aside from this, they consumed many Taco Bell burritos, which were very cheap and filling. Sarah would often lament, "What I wouldn't give for a box of sweet delight, Tim Hortons donuts!"

"I need those like I need a hole in the head," replied Meghan. "We sit all day, hardly moving a muscle."

"What I wouldn't give for a chocolate milkshake right now!" Sarah continued in self-pity.

"I'll buy you a freezie," said Meghan.

"Not even close," retorted her friend.

Meghan was looking into her sun visor mirror. "I'm having a bad hair day," she proclaimed.

"A bad hair day?" replied her friend. "How about a stinky clothes day? Your jeans are really ripe and just because you have a sweatshirt with 'Soccer is my favorite season' printed on it doesn't mean you have to wear it for an entire season. Can't you change into another sweatshirt?"

"You're no sweet pea yourself, you know," replied

Meghan.

"Why are you calling me a sweet pea?"

"I'm not, they actually smell very nice. Unlike you!"

"Hmh."

They were glad they could roll down the windows as the temperatures rose the further south they drove. Every few weeks they would stop at a laundromat, sometimes still wearing their pajamas because all their other clothes really needed to be washed, and get strange looks from patrons of the establishments.

The radio in the camper was broken, so there was no music to listen to. And conversations were limited because of the drone of the tires on the pavement and the loud sound of the motor. Most of their chit-chats took place in little coffee shops along the way. The rest of the time, the driver concentrated on the road and the passenger stared out the window, hoping to see something different and fantastic.

Washington D.C. impressed the two tourists very much. They drove by the White House and waved. They then wandered around a few of the Smithsonian museums. Despite looking like hippies they felt quite refined as they meandered through the museums studying old paintings and admiring works of artists long since passed. After a morning of art education they decided to see the Lincoln Memorial and the Memorial to Vietnam soldiers. They made them feel serene but somber.

A second place that impressed them was Savannah, Georgia. The beautiful parks, cobblestone squares, and large oak trees covered with Spanish moss were remarkable. They drove behind a horse-drawn carriage and took the economy tour. Before they left historic Savannah behind, they went to a diner and shared an order of fried green tomatoes.

"You have a charming accent," Meghan said to the waitress.

"Why honey, I don't have an accent," the waitress lilted. "Y'all have an accent." She winked with one eye and poured more coffee.

As they moved further south, they stopped their camper for the night in some state parks where they didn't have to pay and sometimes on the parking lot of a truck stop. They soon got used to the sound of the big trucks which kept their motors running for hours. One night, they camped on a site on the Alligator Alley which cost a mere $5.00. In the dark of the night, they found a spot. A flashlight barely gave them enough light to find the outhouse. The next morning they noticed a sign which warned "Beware of Alligators."

"It should say, 'Don't feed the alligators'," said Meghan.

"What?" wondered Sarah.

"It's a joke," replied her friend. "What that means is, 'Don't lose your hands and arms to the alligators."

"Very funny."

At the next gas stop the travelers noticed a few cages with small alligators in them. For one dollar they were allowed to take a picture of themselves holding one of these ferocious beasts. They bravely did so because the alligators were not very big and their snouts had been taped shut.

Most campgrounds provided some comfort, showers and fire pits. Sometimes, they joined up a conversation with others, happy to share stories of their travel adventures. At one of these campsites, some trailers were parked permanently. One had a sign on its door "Your Fortunes Told Here."

"Let's do it," said Meghan. "Just for a hoot."

"It's a bunch of bullshit," said Sarah.

"It's actually horseshit," replied Meghan. "The last one I went to said, 'A rich dark stranger will come into your life.' What a lot of crap."

"What's the point? If someone tells you your future then your life is predetermined, you have no free will. I want to control my own destiny."

"Right. So do I, but come on, we need a little excitement! If anything we'll have a good laugh about it."

They entered the premises and saw a woman with long black hair and long painted fingernails. She was using heavy makeup and had dark eyes and ruby-red lips. Multiple bracelets hung on both wrists, earrings dangling and rings on her middle fingers glistened. She looked at the two girls and hesitated a bit before she began. Meghan went first and then Sarah. The fortune teller took her hand and examined the lines on her palm. She looked somewhat perplexed. After some nonsensical drivel, as Meghan saw it, it was now Sarah's turn. The outcome was much the same. She informed both that something terrible would happen in the very near future, but was vague about the details.

As they left the trailer, Sarah spoke: "She creeps me out."

"Are you joking me?" replied Meghan. "She absolutely terrified me in there."

"Maybe that's her thing. But she's not going to get many customers if she keeps telling people what she told us."

"Never mind. Let's not dwell on it," said Meghan. "We've already had a tire trying to escape our camper, a mutinous muffler, and a lot of scrapes and bumps. The condition of your camper is worrisome."

"You're right. I hope that dream catcher dangling from our rear-view mirror will do its job. I don't want any nightmares for the rest of our trip."

Concerned about the things the fortune teller had told them, but trying to laugh it off, they told each other that they would probably be towed more miles by AAA than they would be driving, and look at all the gas they could save that way! The next morning they continued their journey headed west to New Orleans.

Chapter IV

Memphis – Birthplace of Rock'n'Roll and Home of the Blues

"Attention please," said Justin after everyone had made themselves comfortable in their seats. "A couple of hours and we will be in the incredible city of Memphis. We'll be staying in one of the larger hotels and once we're all settled in, we'll get back on the bus and Mike will drive us to Beale Street, the legendary musical haven. We'll be dining in the B.B. King Blues Club. During dinner you'll be listening to some pretty fantastic music. Depending on the night it could be blues, of course, but also soul or rock'n'roll.

"Tomorrow we'll spend half a day at Graceland, Elvis's home. There are so many things to do in Memphis, but we're on a tight schedule. I would have loved to take you to the Sun Studio, the birthplace of rock'n'roll, where Elvis got his start, as did Johnny Cash and Jerry Lee Lewis."

***

The passengers on the bus arrived in Memphis full of anticipation of what the city would offer them. Big Mike took the suitcases out of the lower compartment of the bus and placed them on the pavement. The passengers grabbed their luggage and entered the lobby of an eight-story luxury hotel. They registered and went to their rooms. After an hour, as they had been instructed, they all reassembled in the lobby, congregated there until the coach pulled up. They boarded the bus and were driven to Beale Street.

"All right, people. Quiet please!" shouted the tour guide. "We're going to visit Beale Street, one of Tennessee's most visited attractions. You will hear music streaming from every open door. There are over two dozen bars and nightclubs and a lot of street performers. First of all, we'll be going into the B.B. King Blues Club where we'll have dinner. It's known for its juicy and delicious ribs. So guys, dig in. They also have some signature cocktails, so ladies, please indulge. After dinner you can walk down the street and listen to more music in some of the nightclubs or right on the street, or in the W.C. Handy Park. All I ask is that you return to the top of the street, which is barricaded to traffic, at 11:00 pm. Mike will be parked there and he'll bring you back to the hotel. So, have fun!"

Once on Beale Street they crossed a barrier which was patrolled by the police. The busiest blocks of the street beginning at B.B. King's Blues Club and stretching for a number of blocks were cordoned off to traffic. The group walked into the premises and dispersed in order to find a table for themselves.

***

Four people from Pittsburgh, Pennsylvania, were participating in the Blues Highway Tour. Naomi, a 5′4″ brunette with short wavy hair with streaks of gray, wearing a black and white dress covered by a beige cardigan and comfy shoes was there with her husband, Ben. Their friend Hannah, slightly taller than Naomi, black haired with gray streaks too, dressed in a flowing cotton blouse with cream capris pants and Tretorn canvas shoes, was accompanied by her husband, Larry who had found a table not far from the stage. Two people from the bus asked to join them. Ryder, a tall, soft-spoken man was sporting black jeans and a long-sleeved dark gray collar shirt. His friend Ronny, somewhat shorter, wore blue jeans and a fuchsia t-shirt. His smile was enhanced by dimples on both of his cheeks.

"Wow, you're wearing a hot pink t-shirt," said Larry.

"It's actually fuchsia. I'm a liberated man," replied Ronny.

"Good for you," nodded Larry.

A waitress soon brought them each a menu. "So what will it be, folks?" she asked when she returned after several minutes. It was no big surprise what the tour participants ordered. The guys wanted fatty, juicy ribs. They were already salivating and wishing that this was an 'all you can eat' rib joint, but alas. The women, usually watching their weight, ordered a healthy house salad with dressing on the side.

"And what will you drink with your meal?" asked the waitress.

"A draft," replied Ben. "Blues Brew sounds interesting."

"I'll have a Blue Moon. I mean you've got to have it once, right?" said Larry.

"Very funny," said Ben.

"I'll have one of your signature drinks," said Naomi, reading from the menu. "A Hoochie Coochie Man sounds interesting, 'vanilla vodka, melon liqueur, cranberry and pineapple juice.' Sounds delicious."

"And I'll have a Lucille, 'coconut rum, Blue Curaçao,

orange and pineapple juice'," said Hannah.

"Lucille was the name of B.B. King's guitar, you know," said Ben. "It used to hang on a wall in this restaurant, but it's been sold at an auction. I heard that someone paid $280,000 for it."

"Holy smokes, that's a lot of cash!" said Larry.

A group of people walked into the restaurant and passed their table. One bumped into Ryder. The table shook and his fork bounced and fell onto the floor. He bent over to pick it up, but in that instant Hannah half stood up and shouted at Ryder not to do so.

"There may be all kinds of microorganisms, bacteria or viruses on that floor. Just leave it where it is." She motioned to a waiter to come over and asked for a new fork for Ryder.

"Do you have some kind of germophobia?" he asked, quite astounded by her behavior.

"You might say so. I work in a lab, an almost sterile, germ-free environment."

"Ah." Ryder left the fork on the floor and Hannah sat back down.

"Sorry I was so loud and forceful," said Hannah.

"No worries," replied Ryder.

"You're a blues fan, I gather," said Ronny, sitting beside Hannah, trying to change the subject.

"Well, I do love to listen to it from time to time. Perhaps a song or two from B.B. King, Johnny Rawls or Bonnie Raitt," said Hannah.

"Ah."

"But to be honest, I like jazz a lot better than blues. It's more complex. It has more depth, more originality. I mean, just listen to some of the old vinyls, Ella Fitzgerald, Billy Holiday, Duke Ellington, Miles Davis, Louis Armstrong. Blues is all about repetition, but jazz is about interpretation. An artist never plays a piece the same way twice. Depends on his or her mood," said Hannah.

"And I like more contemporary artists like Wynton Marsalis, Miles Davis, Nina Simone and especially Dianna Krall. Now there is a talent!" added Naomi from across the table.

"I have to agree with you there. Dianna Krall, both talent and good looking," said Ronny. "I myself like both the blues and jazz. I work in a winery in Temecula, California, and every year we have a jazz and blues festival, mostly downtown, but some concerts take place in the vineyards. It's the coolest thing. Good music, good wine, what could be better?"

"I didn't know that," said Hannah, very interested. "Here, I'll give you my phone number and you can text me some info." Turning to Naomi she continued, "What do you think about the four of us flying to California next year to discover the wine-growing regions of California?"

"That sounds great. We can tour vineyards but see other sites as well, swim in the ocean," said Naomi.

"What do you think, Ben?" Naomi asked her husband.

"Sure," he replied. "You and Hannah are usually Larry's and my travel advisers. You haven't been wrong yet."

"That settles it," said Naomi. "We're flying to California next year! Keep the wine chilled, Ronny."

"You bet."

"How about you, Ryder, what do you do, and what kind of music do you like?" asked Larry.

"I work in the IT industry. A lot of people do nowadays.

Not that exciting. As far as music goes, I actually like the Texas Blues, you know, ZZ Top, although I'm not quite sure that it is the blues that they play. I mean they've developed their own style of music."

"That's for sure. Loud, a blues rock band, but good. Thing is, you always like the music that you listened to as a teen. I've always liked Led Zeppelin, Van Halen, Meatloaf, and U2."

"Yes, those are great bands," said Ben. "I used to listen to Nirvana, Pearl Jam, Soundgarden and the Smashing Pumpkins."

"Ah, Grunge. Looking at your attire, you certainly changed then," said Ryder.

"Well, I liked the music but I didn't wear torn or baggy clothes," replied Ben.

"Hey, Ryder, why did you come on this blues trip, if you're not that into the music from around here?"

"Oh, both Ronny and I won free tickets in an online contest."

"You too? So did Naomi and Hannah. What a coincidence!"

"Wow, yeah, it is. Anyways, I'm divorced and just started dating again. Ronny is happily single, so we decided to go on this tour together. We've traveled a lot before, day and weekend trips in our state, California, but once we took a much longer trip on our motorbikes, actually all the way to here."

"Have you been to New Orleans before?"

"Oh yeah."

"Ben and I haven't but Hannah and Naomi have, many moons ago, before they met Ben and me."

"So what do you do, professionally, Hannah?" Ryder

asked.

"I'm a scientist. I work in the Health Care Sciences at the University of Pittsburgh, as a researcher."

"Wow, that's impressive and Naomi, what about you?"

"I'm a naturopathic doctor. My parents tried to put pressure on me and insisted on me becoming a proper MD, but of course, you know the laws of physics," said Naomi, using air quotes as she said the word 'proper.'

"Which laws?"

"For every action there is an equal but opposite reaction. I guess I never liked being told what to do. I always felt constricted and wanted to break free. But don't get me wrong, I love my profession."

"Of course, why wouldn't you? Something to be very proud of," said Ronny. "And how about you, Larry?"

"Oh, I am a dentist. Let me check out your pearly whites," he kidded.

"And you, Ben?"

"Yeah, well, I wasn't as ambitious as my wife. I did go to college to take some business courses. I inherited a furniture business from my dad."

"Good for you, man," said Ronny. "That's the way to do it. I wish my dad would have left me something like that."

✳✳✳

Justin and Mike had made themselves comfortable on the bar stools enjoying some po' boys and drinking a beer. Two people from the bus sat down beside them.

"Where are you from, Justin?" asked a passenger from Chicago who had earlier informed the tour guide that he was a real blues fan and just loved this tour.

"Ah, Seattle," replied Justin.

"Oh, I've never been but I watched the movie," said the man's wife.

"*Sleepless in Seattle*? Yeah, that was very popular."

"Yeah. Seems like a nice city. How long have you been a tour guide?"

"Not that long."

"What did you do before?"

"This and that."

"That's specific," said the man with a bit of sarcasm. Delving further into trying to find out some information, he said: "How about you, Mike. Where are you from?"

"Same as Justin, Seattle."

"So you two have known each other for a while."

"Ah, not that long. We were hired by the tour company around the same time and they gave us this gig."

"So you're a team."

"Right, now we are."

"What did you do before, Mike?"

"Ah, I was a tr—, ah, bus driver."

"But you didn't like it?"

"You know, same route every day, just went around in circles. This is better, nice food, great accommodations and new places to see, a real adventure."

"An upbeat blues journey," said the man from Chicago.

***

Meghan, Will, Sarah and Jim had found a table to sit with others who they did not recognize as passengers on their bus.

"Do you mind if we sit with you?" asked Sarah. "It's

pretty packed in here, eh?"

"Not at all," said an elderly woman. "You're from Canada, I gather."

"Yeah, it's pretty obvious. I've got to stop saying 'eh'."

"No, no, it's kind of cute. Which part of Canada are you from?"

"Niagara."

"Wine country, very nice."

"You've been there?"

"Oh yes, who hasn't been in Niagara Falls. It's one of the most popular tourist destinations in the world, after all."

"I guess. I only see the Falls when we have company."

The restaurant patrons looked at the menus the waitress had brought to the table.

"This looks interesting," said Meghan. "I'll have a cup of Gumbo Yaya. That's very tempting. And I'll have a catfish po' boy and a beer. Is there a particular beer you would suggest that would go well with my dinner?" she asked the waitress.

"I'll have to think on that, better yet, I'll ask the bartender," she replied.

"Thanks."

"And you sir?" asked the waitress looking at Will.

"Ribs and beer."

"Make that two," said Jim.

Meghan ordered three different types of beer.

"Woah there tiger!" said Will. "Easy on the alcohol."

"I'm just trying to see which beer goes best with my dinner."

"Aha."

Meghan looked at Will, raised her eyebrows and started to sing one of her favorite Amy Winehouse songs:

They tried to make me go to Rehab
But I said no, no, no

...

Just try to make me go to Rehab
But I won't go, go, go.

During dinner Meghan nudged Sarah. "You know the guy at the next table, the bald one with the red mustache and goatee..."

Sarah looked over to the table. "Yeah?"

"I think I've seen him before. He looks familiar."

"Really? Where?"

"No clue. Don't know when, either. I think it's his eyes."

"Did you gaze deeply into his big blue eyes? I don't think Will would like that."

"He wouldn't. That's not it. When we were boarding the bus this morning, he looked at me as I was walking by and I noticed that he has eyes that don't match. One is gray blue and the other gray green. That's quite unusual."

"It would be, but maybe you didn't see it right. It was overcast this morning and a little dark in the bus as we were boarding."

"Hm. You sure you've never seen him before?"

"Never."

"Hm."

"You know, I get that all the time. Someone on the street, out of the blue, will say to me, 'Do you have a twin sister?' Either my dad was really busy in his younger years or I have that universal face that everyone recognizes."

"You do not!"

"Think about it. Our city has a population of, what, almost 90,000 people, and yet when I go to an event or the grocery store I don't meet anyone I know and I've lived there all my life. What are the chances of you meeting someone on this trip, or the same bus, when the passengers come from all corners of the States, from Canada, that's us, and, according to Justin, from England and even Australia."

"Guess you're right. What are the chances?"

***

Dylan, Brooke, Jordan and Sally were sitting at a table very close to the raised stage. A young man walked up, introduced himself and started strumming a few tunes. After a while, he began to sing.

"You know, that young guy has a lot of potential," said Dylan.

"He's not bad," said Jordan.

"He really feels the music, you can tell. He's putting a lot of emotion into his songs. He's also playing the classic three-chord scheme, the tonic, subdominant and dominant, returning to tonic. For example the first, fourth and fifth. I could go on."

"No, never mind. We don't know that much about music, just like to listen to it," said Sally.

"In honesty though, shouldn't a blues singer be black? I mean, that is where the music originated, in the cotton fields of the South. It tells of people's trials and tribulations under very harsh conditions, the longing for a better life. It's personal," said Jordan.

"That's the way it started, but you don't necessarily have to be black to experience hardship. A lot of people have demons in their heads, horrible childhoods, soldiers gone to war. You're never the same person when you come back. You could have lost a love, all your money. It goes on and on. If you can sing about it, free your soul from all the terrible things you've experienced, spew it out, you're half way there. Then you don't need a psychiatrist. The music will cleanse you."

"You think? Just don't spew it all over my ribs, okay? I'm still eating."

"Thing is though," added Sally, "once it becomes commercial, once the blues musicians make a lot of money singing, and singing the same songs, is that the true blues? Is that what it's meant to be?"

"No, probably not," said Dylan. "That's why it's so great to see up-and-coming musicians, here in the clubs and out on the streets. They're not making a lot of money, just squeezing by and trying to make a living but passionate about what they're doing and that's what's important."

"I read an article recently that said that the blues is a dying art form, much like Dixieland and Big Band. The music is still performed, but it doesn't have the relevance it once did, especially for younger people," said Jordan.

"That's a real shame," said Dylan.

"So this trip we're taking, it's a kind of nostalgic, historical tour," added Sally.

"Sad, when you think about it," said Brooke.

***

Once the group had finished their dinner and listened to a few blues players, they left the restaurant and walked down Beale Street. Hundreds upon hundreds of people were walking on the cobblestone walkways and also in the middle of the street. Music was drifting out of other restaurants and night clubs, and there was music on the street. A number of small bands or solitary musicians were singing the blues and hoping people would stop to listen, perhaps buy one of their CDs or throw some money into an open guitar case.

The group broke apart and drifted to the music that was of interest to them. Some wanted to dance to DJ music, others were listening to the blues, others to rockabilly at the Jerry Lee Lewis' Café and Honky Tonk. Others yet just stayed on the street watching a group do aerial somersaults, the Beale Street Flippers. A part of the group found their way to a park, not well lit, but it didn't matter. It was a free concert in W.C. Handy Park. On a stage a band was performing some rock music.

***

One by one, the small groups of people meandered back up Beale Street when it got close to 11:00 pm. Their charter bus was waiting to take them back to the hotel. Everyone was in a very good mood. Most went up to their rooms, but others went into the bar of the hotel for a nightcap or two.

"Hey, Ryder," said Ronny, once he had put on his pajamas and was stretched out on his bed in their hotel room. "Do you remember much from the trip we took to New Orleans such a long time ago?"

"You mean, when we were young and foolish, energetic but immature?"

"Yup. Can you remember what year that was?"

"Not really. Let me think."

CHAPTER V

RONNY AND RYDER'S BLUES

We're riding through the desert
The sun is not our friend
We're baking in our leathers
There's tires we have to mend
With flies stuck in our teeth
Cheeks flapping in a gale
Our engines overheating
We hope our bikes won't fail
That's why we're blue, oh yeah
We've got the backroad riding blues

Ryder and Ronny had been friends since kindergarten. They had attended the same elementary and high schools in Orange County, California. Ronny stopped there. He wanted to earn some money, so he started working at a burger joint. Ryder had a bit more ambition and finished one year of college, but the courses he had taken bored him so he decided to take some time off, hit the open road to see where it might lead him. Ronny, by then sick of flipping burgers, decided that this was a great idea, and so he joined his life-long friend on this adventure.

Ryder was a tall, curly black-haired man with dark brown eyes who rode a black 1994, 1100 Honda Shadow Spirit. He thought he looked really cool in his black jeans and black leather jacket, a look emulating his comic book hero *The Shadow*. This masked man with a wide-brimmed black hat, a crimson scarf covering his nose, mouth and chin, and black trench coat, usually with a gun in each hand, was always fighting criminals. A decal of his hero was glued to Ryder's gas tank. Even though he drove a large and powerful bike, the husky young man looked a bit too big for the sporty machine.

He had tightened the chain and put a change of clothes into his tank bag. The minimum amount of weight was of the greatest concern. No room for food or water, only motor oil and some spare parts. Tools were more important. Adjustments had to be made to the suspension. Bolts that would come loose during the trip would have to be tightened.

Ryder drove his bike to Ronny's house. His friend was a few inches shorter, and very thin, with long straight hair tied into a pony tail. Ronny was standing beside his 750 cc, 1993 light blue Honda Shadow, which was similar to Ryder's bike, but somewhat smaller and sleeker. Ronny was listening to a song by Steppenwolf on his transistor radio which he had placed on a table on the front porch. He sang along:

You know I've smoked a lot of grass
Oh, Lord I've popped a lot of pills...

Upon seeing his friend, Ronny turned down the volume.

"Did you fill up your tank or are we going to have to push your bike to the nearest gas station again?" asked Ryder.

"I filled it up last night. No worries. I'm almost ready," replied his friend with a smirk on his face.

"Good," replied Ryder. He brought out a map from his saddle bag and spread it across the hood of one of Ronny's parents' cars.

Looking at a map of the southern United States, he turned to his friend. "Okay. So we're agreed we'll go south on Interstate 5, then east on the 8, then onto Interstate 10 just south of Phoenix."

"Yup. Gotta get as far as possible the first couple of days. I mean, it's almost 2,000 miles from L.A. to New Orleans. If we get bored with the freeway, we can take some secondary roads now and then."

"Right. And then the 90 to San Antonio. From there back on the 10 to New Orleans."

"And Mardi Gras!"

"That's gonna be quite a trip!"

"You said it."

They both put on their helmets and mounted their bikes. It would be a trying and exhausting trip, but freedom was everything. It was a natural high. Both still lived at home with their parents who didn't quite see them as adults just yet. So on this trip there were no parents to make derogatory comments, no curfews, only the challenge to make it from one gas station to the next, the courage to drive fast and perhaps outdo your partner, prove who the best rider was.

There was one rule, no drinking when driving. They didn't need a high from drugs or alcohol. Fumes from the burning oil and gas would have that effect, as did revving the engine at 6 to 7,000 rpms. That sound was addictive.

Food was always the cheapest they could find, hot dogs, burgers and a Coke. At one of the truck stops where they refueled their gas tanks and themselves, they met other bikers. One group they met they considered to be just show-offs. It seemed wherever Ronny and Ryder had been, they had been too, and in a lot of other places as well.

"Have you ever been to..." Ryder began.

"Been there, seen that, and bought the t-shirt," said one of the bikers condescendingly.

It seemed as if these guys didn't ride to a place to enjoy the scenery, they wanted high odometer readings and impress other riders.

Ryder and Ronny stopped in many small towns, mostly to fill up their gas tanks and grab a soda. The questions and comments from some of the elderly people who seemed to like sitting on benches outside the general store were generally the same.

"Great-looking bikes, boys," said one of the old-timers.

"Where you from and where you headed?" asked another.

"So how long is it gonna take you to get to New Orleans?"

The boys answered some of those questions but they themselves did not know how long their trip would last. It depended on so many variables, weather, road conditions, dependability of their bikes and their own stamina, to mention a few.

They each grabbed a beverage and chatted with the old men. They were happy to show off their fabulous bikes and talk about how powerful they were. Realizing that the old folks were not that tech-savvy, they talked about their end destination, Mardi Gras in New Orleans. The old men nodded and said they would love to go there themselves were they but a few years younger. Nowadays, they were happy to live these adventures vicariously through the stories told by younger folks.

One of their stops was on an Arizona Indian reservation.

An elderly man with a tanned, wrinkled, leathery-looking face, straight, long gray hair, looked at the two riders with an odd expression on his face. Ryder wondered if he perhaps was a spiritual and physical healer.

"Do you think we should ask him for some peyote?" Ronny whispered to Ryder.

"Don't say something like that. Sometimes I'm not sure if you're kidding or being serious."

The old man said something very vague but disconcerting: "Your innocence will not set you free."

"What the hell did that mean?" the boys were thinking.

And then he added, "You should turn around and ride back home."

Ronny and Ryder looked at one another. Who was this man to tell them what to do? He was not their grandfather. They had a plan, a journey's end in mind. They were going to reach their destination, come hell or high water. Since they were riding through the desert they didn't fear high water, so there was only one thing that made them uneasy, the hell that could be the desert.

They left the reservation and continued in an eastward direction. At times, riding was surviving a very real and dangerous obstacle course. Shredded tires from trucks were strewn across the lanes of the freeway. Dark, very slippery patches of liquefied tar would appear in the extreme heat of the desert and bubble up to the surface. These slippery patches had to be traversed very carefully. And then the dust storms which would blow in without warning, at times reducing visibility to a few feet. Stopping during one of these storms was almost impossible as a truck or car rear-ending and thereby really ending them was a possibility.

They had been traveling for several days already and were now in New Mexico. The two motorcycle riders decided to take a break from the constant stress of heavy traffic, those big trucks flying by that would sometimes box them in on the expressway. Ryder suggested they take a relaxing ride on a secondary road. The pace was slower, the road winding and therefore more fun to ride and they could actually enjoy the beautiful scenery.

After an hour of riding bliss, they were suddenly passed by a caravan of oddly shaped cars on the other lane of the road. There were no identifying marks as to what type of cars they were. They could not look into the side windows. These had been taped with something and the windshields were tinted.

Ryder and Ronny stopped at the side of the road deciding if they should follow these strange cars to get a closer look at the weirdly shaped vehicles that looked like squashable bugs.

"Did you see that?" asked Ronny.

"What do you think they were?" replied his partner.

"Earth buggies from a UFO that landed a few miles from here."

"Did you smoke some weed this morning when I was still sleeping?"

"No man, I'm sticking to our rules, no reefers until we get to New Orleans where we won't be riding our bikes for a few days."

"In that case, is there a history of mental illness in your family?"

"No more than in yours."

"Very funny."

"Seriously, think about it. We're in the desert, not that

far from Roswell. The government captured a UFO many years ago and kept the aliens in an underground bunker."

"You've been watching too many sci-fi flicks."

"Well then, what? The vehicles looked camouflaged. Do you think they were military?"

"No, wasn't army camouflage, and the army wouldn't have vehicles looking like turtles."

"So what were they?"

"Probably a test drive for a new prototype of car. Maybe the manufacturer is still re-designing it."

"I could give them a few pointers. Let's get back to the freeway. I don't want to come across anything else that's weird out here."

Ryder looked at his map of New Mexico. "Another half an hour before we hit Route 285 that will take us south to Texas and back on Interstate 10. There should be a gas station at the next crossing."

Finding a gas station in time was always on their minds. The drone of the freeway, constantly shifting gears, watching for loose gravel on secondary roads, the washboard surface of some roads gouged by heavy trucks, hanging on tight to wiggling handle bars and the parched, hot, dry air made them tired. After a day's ride of around 400 miles they were sore and they looked for a place to rest their tired bodies. It was always a cheap, low-end motel. The bikes would be gassed up, dead bugs would be wiped off their helmets and they would eat some greasy food, park their bikes right in front of their motel windows and crash on their lumpy, uncomfortable beds.

The next morning would be the same as the day before, get up early, eat breakfast, and make good mileage before it got too hot. They would continue this sometimes terrifying yet inexplicably exhilarating trip. And with a twist of the throttle they would unleash a burst of power in their magnificent machines.

CHAPTER VI

GRACELAND –
"PURE AMERICANA,

center of the American universe, I mean, the Kennedys may have been the American royal family, but Elvis was the true king, King of rock'n'roll, but also King of the United States," said Jim.

"You really think so?" asked Will.

"Hell yeah. He conquered the whole world with his music at a time when America was the true leader of the entire world, when they had unrivaled power and prestige. People in other countries were in awe and wanted to be just like them. On the European continent women wore nylons, just like the women in America. Kids chewed gum for the first time and men had their hair slicked back like Elvis and wore side burns. Even now, so many years after his death, how many Elvii are there impersonating him? I bet everyone in the world has seen one, especially the Las Vegas Elvis with his rhinestone-covered sparkly jumpsuits."

"I think Michael Jackson was a far greater talent. Elvis had a great voice, but Michael wrote all his own songs. Elvis just sang other people's songs. Admittedly, there was a great deal of variety. He sang rock'n'roll, of course, but also country, gospel and Christmas songs. Something for everyone, I guess."

"Yeah, he also starred in numerous movies."

"One like the other. All cloned, and embarrassingly bad."

"All right, all right, you guys. Stop it. Let's just enjoy walking through the King's home," said Sarah.

The group was impressed as they were herded through the mansion sitting on almost fourteen acres of land. This king's castle had twenty-three rooms, including eight bedrooms and bathrooms, a jungle room with a waterfall. Also, his memorabilia was displayed in the Trophy Building, his gold and platinum records, his popular outfits during his Las Vegas years, his uniform worn during his stint in the army, and even his wedding tuxedo. Elvis, a poor boy born in Tupelo, Mississippi, had been the embodiment of the American Dream. He came from nothing to become something. Graceland was a showcase of his material wealth and proof of his success. He was an icon, an inspiration to those who had that same dream.

"I'm anxious to see Elvis's resting place in the Meditation Garden," said Meghan.

The group made its way through the estate, the mansion, the automobile museum, one of the airplanes, and several gift shops. In one of the shops the background music was the king crooning a love song, *Kismet.*

When you meet by chance, it's not by chance
It's kismet
...
Until you came by, kismet and I were strangers
But now that you're here, it's suddenly clear we've met

"I've heard a lot of Elvis's songs, but never this one. What does 'kismet' mean? Is it actually a word?" asked Jim.

"It means fate, your destiny," Sarah enlightened her husband.

"Sounds weird. With all the songs that Elvis ever record-ed you'd think they would play a better one. Oh well." He took a shirt off a rack, looked at it and smiled. He bought himself a black t-shirt imprinted with a pink Cadillac, one of Elvis's many cars.

***

Back on the bus, Justin began to speak about their next des-tination, Clarksdale. "I hope everyone enjoyed Graceland. I know many of you would have liked to spend more time there, but we have a pretty full agenda and a tight schedule today. We're off to Clarksdale which is about eighty miles from here and will take us about one and a half hours of driving.

"This is where the blues originated, with Robert Johnson. We're going to drive to the legendary Crossroads, the in-tersection of Highways 49 and 61, although some people say it was actually a few miles out of town. Of course, at that time, almost a century ago, it was open country and no one saw what really happened. It is said that Johnson made a pact with the devil so that he could play his guitar better than any other man alive."

There were many whispers in the bus. "Here we go," said Ronny. "Let's get a good look at this legendary, su-pernatural place."

"Perhaps we could have a little chit chat with Satan him-self," replied Ryder with bit of sarcasm.

"I think you have to make an appointment first," kidded Ronny.

"Ah, I didn't know, would that be over the telephone or online?"

"Everything's online nowadays. We could book fifteen minute individual meetings or perhaps have a grand parley as a group."

"You're a hoot."

"You go ahead Ryder. I'll be out there in a minute, just want to change into something else."

"So you need an appointment and proper attire to meet the devil?" kidded his friend.

Justin smiled at everyone as they were exiting the bus and informed them that they would be stopping in the restaurant parking lot for twenty minutes. "That will be plenty of time for everyone to go out and take a picture of yourselves and the three giant blue guitars. And, if anyone has the desire to become the absolute best in something," he added, "you know what to do." He paused for a moment and then said, almost to himself, "Just kidding."

People stepped out of the bus and walked onto the little patch of green between two paved roads and a parking lot and took a lot of pictures with their smart phones and iPads.

"I can't believe you're still wearing your flip-flops," Will said to his wife.

"They're super comfy," said Meghan.

"I realize that, but I was sure one of those oafs in the lineup back at Graceland was going to step on your toes when he began pushing us forward."

"Should I wear steel-capped boots, like I do at work?"

Will rolled his eyes.

"So this is it, Ground Zero," said Dylan.

"I think that's in New York City," Brooke corrected her husband.

"I'm aware of that, but this is ground zero for the blues, the beginning, the birth, the origin."

"It's a very special place. I'm experiencing an epiphany right now," said Sally.

"Let me know what that's like. I want to be enlightened," kidded Jordan.

"What do you think of this place, Justin?" asked Ryder who was standing beside the tour guide.

He thought for a moment, "I think it's too basic, three blues guitars on a street pole. There should be more adoration, some plaques, music playing, a larger park..."

"I agree. I mean it's so small, three bushy trees, a few shrubs and a bit of grass, a yield sign and some telephone poles. I think they could do better for a place that is so important. The music that originated here has circled the whole earth and inspired so many musicians besides blues artists."

"If you want to hear music in this place you'll have to come back at midnight. Legend has it that the devil walks here with a guitar in hand. Perhaps you can ask him to play a few tunes."

"Do you think a ghost-like image of the devil will appear in the background of our pictures of this place?" asked Sarah.

"Don't be daft, this is the Crossroads. It will be an image of the devil, demons, evil spirits, fiends, monsters and werewolves, a devilishly great blues band, howling out their satanic music," said Jim.

"Oh, you mean like 'Smooth'", replied his wife.

"I said satanic music, not Santana."

"Oh, you're right. That would be Santanic music," replied Sarah, with a grin.

"I think you're both nuts," said Meghan, passing her two friends as she stepped back into the bus.

***

"There you have it folks, that was the Devil's Crossroads. Oh, and Ronny, great t-shirt, The Stones and their *Sympathy for the Devil* album cover imprinted on it. Very apropos. Clarksdale gave birth to the blues. It also gave birth to famous blues entertainers like John Lee Hooker, Ike Turner and Muddy Waters. I'd love to take you to Indianola, which isn't far away and is the birthplace of B.B. King. There is a B.B. King Museum and Interpretive Center, and the man himself is buried in the back of the museum, but sadly there isn't enough time. Perhaps the next time you come down this way, you can go to all the interesting places we missed.

"You must all be starving right about now. I have a great place lined up. We're going to be having a late lunch at the Ground Zero Blues Club, which, by the way, is co-owned by Morgan Freeman. He's actually one of my favorite actors. He's been in so many great movies. I'm sorry that there won't be any music, there is none playing at this time, only for dinner."

The building, which from the outside looked like a two-story warehouse, appeared run down, really rough. Red paint was fading and peeling off. Something that was once painted on the facade was now illegible. According to some sources it had once been used as a grocery store. The inside had not been remodeled and now had the authentic ambiance of a juke joint. There was no particular decor, just long tables with different kinds of plastic tablecloths, mismatched chairs, Christmas tree lights strung across the ceiling and graffiti everywhere on the walls. It wasn't very pretty, but a place where local musicians had a chance to work regularly. For a true blues fan this was a sacred place.

Inside the restaurant everyone found a place to sit down at the long, communal tables. A waiter brought the menu.

"I'm going to have the Miss Delta Taco, flap jacks filled with pulled pork. So, Mustang Sally, what'll it be?" asked Dylan who was sitting right beside her.

"I've told you a million times not to call me that. I've never driven a Mustang. I drove a red Daytona when Jordan and I met."

"I would like a Delta Catfish Dinner," said Jordan. "I hope it doesn't taste too earthy."

"What?" asked Sally.

"They're bottom feeders, probably swallow a lot of mud."

"Then order something else," said his wife.

"I'll have the Crossroads Burger," said Brooke. "Seems appropriate in this place."

"Well, going along with that I'll have the Highway 61 Burger," said Sally.

"You know, I've been thinking about the song they were playing in the gift shop, 'Kismet', fate," Meghan said to her friend Sarah who was sitting beside her.

"Do you think it's fate that our whole group heard that song?" asked Sarah.

"No, I'm wondering if it's fate that we're all on this tour," replied Meghan.

"What exactly are you trying to say? It's fate that all thirty-four people met?"

"It's actually thirty six with the tour guide and bus driver. I'm not really sure what exactly I'm trying to get at. In the Elvis movie fate brings two lovers together. But, you and I are already married, and I'm wondering is fate always a positive thing?"

"Probably not. Do you remember on our not so little Westfalia excursion way back when, I didn't want to see that psychic in Florida because if you believe that shit, your life is predetermined and I want control over my future. In the same way, if fate determines our futures then we have no life choices. We're doomed to either be happy or sad."

"Terrified or dead."

"Hmh. Kind of sucks when you think about it."

Before some of the passengers left the restaurant, they passed around a felt-tipped pen and added their names to the many already scribbled on the walls.

✳✳✳

After a satisfying lunch, the group continued on their journey. "We're off to Natchez, which is a four-hour drive, so get comfy and relax. We'll be arriving well into the evening. Our stay will be at the Natchez Grand Hotel, a very prestigious four-story red-bricked hotel with all the comforts you need, including a fitness center, a whirlpool hot tub, wireless high speed internet access and an outdoor pool. The hotel is located on a bluff with a beautiful view of the Mississippi River.

"Natchez has more antebellum architecture than any other city in the South. For those of you who don't know what antebellum means, it means before the war, before the Civil War 1861–1865, of course. When you think of that kind of architecture, it is the big elegant plantation mansions with large Greek columns supporting an over-sized balcony, complemented by enormous entrances, that come to mind. It reminds me of the classic movie *Gone with the Wind*."

"I don't give a damn, Scarlett," Jim shouted.

"Very funny," said Sarah, with a bit of sarcasm.

Justin smiled at the little joke. "We won't be having supper at the hotel but in a restaurant which is within walking distance from the hotel and is right on the river. Has a great menu. There's also a casino, if anyone is interested in going there after supper."

✱✱✱

Passengers sat back comfortably in their seats, ready to enjoy their next destination. After driving for half an hour, Jordan turned to Sally. "You know when Dylan called you Mustang Sally, it brought back memories."

"What memories?"

"You know, when we met and you were driving your hot car. A hot chick in a hot car. How could I resist. And you were a poet to boot."

Sally smiled. "Ah, yes, the song I wrote about my car.

Don't know if I still remember all the words."
  "You should know the lyrics, you wrote them."
  "Yeah, but that was so long ago."
  "I think that I still remember," said Jordan.
  "Then sing with me," said his wife. They both began:

Sally: I've got a flaming hot Daytona
Jordan: *My oh my*
S: I've got the speed to knock you over
J: *Passing by*
        I've got a sunny disposition
        That's very nice
        I'm singing Whitney's new rendition
        Once or twice
        What good are all the things I've got here
        And here's the bad news
        I've got the Monday morning working blues
Both: Monday morning working blues

S: I should be cruisin' down the highway
J: *In your car*
S: I'm sayin' baby goin' my way
        Don't go too far
        I've got to do an exploration
        What's your plan
        I need a permanent vacation
        If you can
        But I can't go, I've obligations
        Ain't it the truth
        I've got the Monday morning working blues
B: Yeah, yeah, Monday morning working blues.

Well you can take this job and shove it
Wherever you please
Or get somebody else who loves it
Should be a breeze
Can't stand to work the first and last day
Of the week
It's time that life start going my way
'Cause you're unique
I need to find a sugar daddy
Who's long overdue
I've got the Monday morning working blues
Yeah, *yeah, Monday morning working blues.*

When Sally and Jordan began singing, Justin turned off the music playing over the intercom, jumped up onto the aisle and walked toward the two singers. Once they had finished their impromptu blues contribution to this trip, he applauded them.

"That was very good guys. Bravo. Do we have any other talented people on this bus?" He looked ahead and behind him. "Come on!"

"I'll play a song," said an elderly gentleman. He took a mouth organ out of his shirt pocket and began to play and sing 'Sweet Home Chicago.'

"Very nice, man," said Dylan. "Loved *The Blues Brothers.* Do you know any other blues songs? How about B.B. King's 'The Thrill is Gone'?"

"I do. Let me see." He began, alternating between singing and playing a few bars on his instrument.

"Why did you ask him to play that one in particular?" asked Brooke. "Are you trying to say something to me?"

"No, baby. It's just a classic blues song that I love to hear.

I think it's one of the best blues ever recorded. B.B. King's raspy, wailing voice accompanied by his weeping guitar is just mind-blowing."

"Aha."

He was lying to his wife and to himself. He wanted to leave her, but couldn't. They had a son whom he loved very much and he didn't want him torn between the two parents. He had a large business, half of which he did not want to fork over to an ex-wife. He had never loved Brooke. He had only married her because she was pregnant, an honorable thing to do, he had thought. But she jabbered and nattered and annoyed him to no end. Alcohol was his escape. For short moments, he could drown her out and live in a quiet, serene parallel world.

***

"Larry, how about switching seats?" Naomi said to her friend across the aisle.

"Sure. No probs." He stepped into the aisle and let Naomi sit beside his wife. He sat beside Ben.

"Hey girl, you look a little tired," said Naomi.

"I know, I'm exhausted," replied Hannah.

"Why?"

"I've been working on this experiment and been in the lab day and night lately. It's a good thing that Larry is so good with the kids. He actually picked me up at the university just an hour before we had to be at the airport for our flight to Nashville."

"He's a great guy."

"Yup."

"Do you remember in high school when we had a few

little explosions in the chemistry labs for which we were reprimanded? But man, it was fun! We both thought we were mad scientists and that we would find a cure for some disease or other and receive Nobel Prizes for medicine."

"Yeah, well I don't have my hopes high on that."

"Why not? You have done some amazing research and a couple of your peer-reviewed articles in pretty prestigious scientific journals have been referenced by not one, but two scientists who have won a Nobel Prize. That in itself is pretty awesome."

"Well, that's about as close as I'm ever gonna get to one of those prizes."

"Don't say that, you still have a lot of years ahead of you and you work in an amazing environment at Pitt."

"I'm not in it for the glory, you know, Naomi. I really want to make a difference, find something that will help mankind."

"And womankind, childrenkind, infantkind, etcetera."

"You dork, but yes, you're right. All right, different topic. Naomi, do any of these places we've just passed bring back memories to you?"

"Sure do. We traveled some of these roads on our trip back from our eventful excursion in my old Beetle."

"Do you still drive that old love bug?"

"I do, but only a couple of miles each summer. Don't ask me why, but I just love it. Can I pick you up for a ride some day?"

"Mmh, no. A ride in that jalopy wouldn't have anything to do with comfort."

"No, but it might bring back a lot of memories."

"Of that one February when we drove south..."

Chapter VII

Hannah and Naomi's Blues

We're slidin' on icy pavement
And hope the snow will melt
To drive this '68 Beetle
Is the scariest we've ever felt
No profile on the tires
No heat inside the cab
And brakes that work so squeakily
This trip might turn out bad
That's why we're blue, oh yeah
We've got the slidin' backroad blues

Naomi and Hannah had met in their junior year of high school. Their parents had moved to Squirrel Hill, Pittsburgh, during that summer, Naomi's parents in July and Hannah's parents in August. Hannah's father had opened a pharmacy on Murray St. and Naomi's mother had accepted a tenure track position at Carnegie Mellon, in the Biology Department.

The two girls were the newbies in all the classes and soon became the best of friends. Hannah, a little taller than her friend, had jet black hair and warm dark-brown eyes. Naomi was a bright young girl with intelligent eyes. They were not interested in, or very good at, for that matter, sports and therefore did not join any school teams. They also had no desire, actually they were never asked, to be in any of the school sororities.

Their passion was science. Labs were always the highlight of each day for the two classmates. No matter how much the teacher tried to instill safety guidelines to the class, Hannah's beakers and test tubes would spew with an eruption any volcano would envy. On Naomi's Petri dishes metals such as potassium would bubble and wildly dance to the rhythm of a Latin beat in her head, because she had once again added too large a chunk of the metal. In other experiments, plumes of smoke would rise high into the air and cloak everything and everyone nearby. Fire would keep fit by doing jumping jacks on her counter top and then hop-scotch over to the next working station.

After one too many smoke alarms had gone off and the entire class would, once again, have to evacuate the building, Hannah and Naomi were sent to the vice principal's office. Feigning a look of innocence, they explained that they thought they had followed the teacher's directions and couldn't comprehend what had gone wrong in their lab. And on top of all that, it was totally unfair that they had to stay for a detention after school.

Science teachers began to monitor the two mad scientists and watched them closely. The only "accidents" from then on occurred when other students had problems with their lab work and the teacher had to venture over to the far side of the classroom. Teachers were annoyed with the over-zealous students, but couldn't say very much. Hannah and Naomi had exceptionally good grades and had visions of winning a Nobel Prize sometime in the future.

They were quite confident that they knew into which field of study they would be venturing and they also knew that a mere four-year degree from a university was not enough for their parents. They insisted on an MD or a PhD. Having worked so hard in high school and knowing that there were many years of hard studies ahead, Naomi and Hannah decided to take a year off, a sabbatical of sorts. They had been accepted at highly regarded universities but intended to defer for one year. It had been hard to convince their parents, who naturally believed that their daughters, once out of school, would never go back and that their fate would be to spend their lives flipping burgers or serving coffee and donuts. Hannah besought her parents. She pleaded with them and tried to convince them that this would be a great life experience. Naomi simply fainted when the discussion with her parents was headed in the wrong direction. Well, she didn't really. Her supposed loss of consciousness was worthy of an Oscar, or perhaps an Emmy, nomination.

In their year of freedom, the two girls flew to Europe. They spent four weeks, two in Italy and two in France, WWOOFing. For food and lodging they worked on organic farms as willing workers, gardening, feeding livestock and weeding for five to six hours a day. They met many students from other countries who were also volunteer WWOOFers, learning how to grow food in a sound ecological way. Once they had completed their four-week obligations, Hannah and Naomi took to the road. They backpacked their way through Italy, Switzerland and Germany, sleeping in youth hostels and on overnight trains.

Naomi had one city she really wanted to visit, Wolfsburg in Germany. This was the headquarters of the mighty manufacturer of the dwarf-sized Volkswagen. Since her father had bought her a 1968 Volkswagen Beetle the past year, Naomi's wish was to see the factory where these classic cars were built, but more so the Museum in the Dieselstrasse which displayed the beautifully awkward-looking vehicles.

The two young travelers had flown back to Pittsburgh in time for Hanukkah, to spend time with their families to enjoy brisket stew, latkes, kugel and jelly-filled donuts. But in the New Year, they both got itchy feet again.

"What do you say we drive down to New Orleans, for Mardi Gras in February?" Naomi asked her friend.

"In that old jalopy of yours? Why do you even drive that car?" responded Hannah. "And why do you have two little flying pigs hanging from your rear-view mirror?"

"First of all, it's not a jalopy. It's a classic, a 1968 Volkswagen Beetle. I fell in love with the bug when I saw a Disney movie, *Herbie*."

"Aha. But it's not in mint condition, though, that's for sure."

"I try to repair my car when it squeaks and rattles, and when I have some money. And, to answer your second question, my piglets are motivational. If pigs can fly, then anything is possible. I can be anything and I can do anything."

"Okay. I don't understand why anyone would drive a standard in Pittsburgh, especially in Squirrel Hill. I mean, how do you even start it on a hill? I bet you've hit a number of cars behind you just trying to clear an intersection."

"One or two, I won't lie." Pause. "Perhaps a dozen."

"Does sound great though."

"What?"

"Mardi Gras."

"Should we book a hotel?"

"Don't think so. I mean, I do have confidence in my car, but who knows how long it will take us to get down there."

"Or if.

"You're right. Let's plan out our route and even if we don't make it all the way to New Orleans, well, at least we'll have fun being on the road, meeting all kinds of people."

"Yeah, truck drivers from AAA, mechanics in garages, ambulance attendants…"

"Oh, stop it!"

"It will be an experiment of sorts, though. Let's see, you add one part Beetle, one part snowstorm, one part icy roads, one part large trucks passing us and spewing wet slush on our windshield and what have you got?"

"An adventure."

"Just make sure your breaks are working and the tires have some profile."

"Yes, Ma'am."

The young high school graduates looked over a road map of the United States in Naomi's bedroom. "We could take the 376 to the 79 and head towards West Virginia, the 64 to Lexington, then the 75 to Chattanooga. I want to start singing 'Chattanooga Choo Choo' every time I hear that word."

"You're too young to know that song. Actually, your parents are too young to know it."

"Must have watched an old movie. And then the 59 to New Orleans."

"Ah. The route you want to follow is all major highways. Are you sure that's the route you want to take?"

"I know secondary roads are more interesting but it is

February. I don't want to end up in the mountains. We should aim for flat terrain and go as far south as we can in as short a time possible so we don't have to worry about icy roads."

"I think another route is better. Let's take the 376 to the 79, then the 70 to Columbus, Ohio, the 71 to Louisville, south on the 65 to the 40 to Memphis and the 55 to New Orleans. On our way back home we can take some secondary roads the first day. There won't be any ice or snow to worry about."

"You're right. That makes a whole lot more sense."

The girls packed what they thought they needed for cold and warm weather. They had checked and found out that the average temperature in New Orleans at this time was in the mid-sixties Fahrenheit.

***

Once on the freeway, Naomi drove her little bug at a constant speed of 50 mph. She always stayed in the right lane and was passed by countless cars and trucks. Since she only had a ten-gallon gas tank she had to fill up every 200 miles or so. The Bug was buzzing along. Hannah tuned in to a popular jazz station on the radio. An announcer expressed great delight in playing the next song. It was Benny Golson's "I Remember Clifford." The jazz enthusiast Hannah hummed along, as did the speakers connected by a loose wire.

At 2:00 p.m. they noticed several large billboards at the side of the road boasting about the great food served in a place a few miles off the highway. Tucky's Best served fried green tomatoes, fried okra, chicken and dumplings, country ham burgoo, barbecued meats and pecan pie.

"Mmh, pecan pie! That's for me," said Hannah.

Naomi exited from the highway but let her friend know that she felt a little uneasy about doing so.

"It's okay, Naomi," said Hannah, "we don't have to eat at truck stops off the freeway. I'm sure we'll be able to find our way back to the interstate once we're finished eating."

"Oh, stop it."

"Tucky's parking lot was overflowing, which was a very good sign. This seemed to be a very popular spot to dine, so the food had to be good. They entered the restaurant and were assigned a table for two by a window. It was always reassuring to be able to see one's vehicle safe and sound in a parking spot.

The waitress brought two menus and two glasses of water. After a few minutes she returned. "What'll it be, girls?" she asked.

"I'll have the chicken and dumplings," said Hannah.

"And I'll have the burgoo. It's not too spicy, is it?"

"I can ask the cook to go easy on the hot sauce."

"And for dessert, we'll both have pecan pie and a coffee."

"Sounds good. Would you like some coffee right now?"

"Sure."

As they were sitting and talking about the morning's drive and how much further they could coerce their little vehicle, a very large man in scraggly, unkempt hair, a checkered shirt and dirty, baggy overalls sat down at the table beside the girls. Hannah noticed that some of his front teeth were missing.

"I'll have the usual, Susie," he said.

The girls enjoyed their meals and were anxiously awaiting the pecan pie. Naomi decided to go to the restroom so she wouldn't have to make a pit stop along their way before they reached their day's destination. While she was gone the man stood up and walked over to Hannah.

"Where are you two young ladies going?" he asked.

"South," she replied not wanting to give away too much information.

"Don't continue the road trip!" he said. "Not a good idea. You should turn around and go back home to Pennsylvania. That is your little Volkswagen Beetle out there, isn't it? Noticed your license plate."

"Yes," she replied.

Hannah was dumbfounded. The man walked to the counter and paid for his meal and then left the restaurant. Hannah told Naomi of the weird conversation she had just had with the hillbilly.

"Who is that man?" Hannah asked the waitress when she came over to their table with the bill.

"Oh, never mind him. Woody's been into his hooch again. He's a Vietnam veteran. Once he came back from that war he was never quite right again. He also drinks far too much of his homemade moonshine. He probably also grows his own marijuana. Real shame! Seems to think he's found his own portal into the future. What did he say to you?"

"Oh, doesn't matter," said Hannah. But it did seem to matter. Hannah couldn't stop thinking about what he had said, for the next few days and for years thereafter.

Chapter VIII

Natchez – Oldest City on the Mississippi River

Bags were unloaded and everyone received the keys to their rooms. Justin had told everyone to take an hour and then assemble in the lobby. They would all walk over to an amazing restaurant right on the Mississippi River.

"This city should be called Lady Antebellum," said Jim.

"What?" asked Will.

"It has so much antebellum architecture."

"Lady Antebellum is a country music group. Well, that's what they used to call themselves. Now their name has been changed to Lady A."

"Why's that?"

"A lot of people think it's politically incorrect, insensitive because 'antebellum' reminds them of a dark period of time in the southern U.S. history, the time of slavery."

"I see."

"Yeah, the Dixie Chicks also dropped 'Dixie' from their name recently. Same reason."

"Makes sense."

"Yeah, I agree," added Meghan. "Some professional teams are also thinking of dropping indigenous names, the Washington Redskins, for instance."

"Do we have any such team names in Canada?" asked

Sarah.

"Used to, but not any more. We do have the features of a First Nations woman on one of the team's logos in the senior lacrosse league association," said Jim.

"What are you, a walking Wikipedia?" asked his wife.

"I like lacrosse."

***

The group had re-assembled in the lobby of the hotel. A short walk and they were in a restaurant right at the edge of the Mississippi River. It was built in an area, Justin had informed them, that used to be a steamboat landing wharf, a very rough neighborhood with gamblers and drunkards. Now, however, the building had been refurbished for people who wanted a wonderful but casual dining experience. The food was great and the glassed-in deck offered a spectacular view of the Mississippi River rolling along. As the sun went down, the great ball of fire sank behind a bridge spanning the river. Everyone took out their smart phones to take a photo of this impressive scene. The staff was friendly and soon, everyone was choosing a meal from the menu.

"Did you see the smile on Justin's face as we walked into the restaurant?" Hannah asked her friend Naomi.

"Yeah?"

"It's fake."

"Of course it's fake. He's not our friend, he's our tour guide. He's been trained by his company to be friendly to the passengers, even if they're obnoxious."

"True. But even so, it's really fake. Reminds me of one

of my co-workers who was always so grumpy and nasty to other workers. The university actually forced her to take some sensitivity training so that she would be more friendly to her co-workers. One day last week, she passed me in a hallway and smiled at me. I just about had a heart attack. I had that same sick feeling just now."

"You're not going to have one right now, are you? Remind me to never smile at you again so that you won't have a myocardial infarction."

"I will. If you've watched him, he doesn't have a lot of eye contact. Usually talks over the passengers, not to them."

"Well, to be honest, there isn't a lot of eye contact between anyone anymore. People talk to you at the dinner table, but they're staring into their iPhones, and teenagers, don't get me started on that!"

"You know what I would like?" Meghan said to Will.

"What's that?"

"Real southern cooking, fried chicken and a peach cobbler. I've read that it goes really well with a refreshing light lager."

"Oh, I would go for that. Let me look at the menu to see if they serve it."

The menu was diverse, a lot of seafood such as catfish and shrimp, but also rib eye steaks. For dessert there was chocolate pecan pie or homemade coconut buttermilk pie.

"Can we join you?" asked Larry who didn't see any empty tables in the restaurant.

"Be our guests," answered Meghan.

"Thanks," said Naomi who, with Hannah and Ben, joined the group.

"So you're from Canada. I overheard a couple of

conversations, not that I'm nosy or anything," said Larry.

"Yes, we are," said Meghan.

"Being on this trip, you guys are blues fans, I gather," said Hannah.

"I listen to the blues once in a while, but when I'm working I have smooth jazz playing in the background. I find it very relaxing," replied Meghan. "To be honest, I don't really have any favorite musicians or bands. I really like 70s disco music of which the Bee Gees are most memorable, but I'm also fond of 80s synthesizer music and 90s dance music."

"So you only came on the tour because you got free tickets, like us. I wonder how many of these passengers did. I wonder who's paying for all of this? Must cost a fortune. What's in it for them? Surely not out of the goodness of their hearts? There's got to be a catch," said Hannah.

"That's ridiculous," said Naomi. "People win things all the time, like in the lottery."

"I've been playing weekly for twenty years and only ever win ten dollars or a free ticket."

"Well, now you've won the jackpot."

"Hmh. I wonder."

From conversations on the bus and in restaurants it seemed that Dylan was one of only a few people who were true blues fans in the group. Hannah and Naomi were true jazz enthusiasts and were therefore excited to win this trip which would take them to New Orleans, the birthplace of their favorite music. Everyone else had heard a few blues tunes now and then but clearly wasn't particularly into that genre of music. And yet they allowed themselves to be deeply immersed in the blues experience. For three days, they would be inundated with blues music on the bus and on Beale Street, by going to blues clubs, restaurants and a juke joint. They stopped at historical blues sites, were given unending facts about historical events and places of significance by the tour guide. As a matter of fact, several drowned out the blues music coming over the audio system on the bus with their own genre on their electronic devices. So why did they put themselves into this situation when they were clearly not that interested in this music? Why participate in this road trip? Only because of a free ticket they or their partner had won?

"It wasn't so much that this is a blues excursion that got Will and me excited about this trip, more than anything it's the southern cooking," said Meghan "We own a craft brewery in a little village in the Niagara Peninsula. We want to sample different foods and see which southern dishes pair well with our beer. Our aim is to expand the menu of our little restaurant. Find a niche to attract customers."

"Right now, we're only serving peanuts, cheese sandwiches, some with prosciutto and pesto, cured meats and cheese on crackers," said Will.

"I see," said Hannah.

"We've already sampled some dishes back in Memphis and Clarksdale and spoke with some of the waiters and waitresses and asked their opinion. Here on the menu they're offering gumbo and saying that it goes well with brown ales, bock lager, or English Porter. The maltiness of these beers are somewhat sweet and create a good balance that contrasts with this spicy dish," said Will.

"Seems you're well on your way in developing a menu for your pub," said Hannah.

"Oh yeah. This trip has been fantastic. Will and I are

hoping to get a lot more recipes in New Orleans. It's a Cajun and Creole culinary heaven," replied Meghan. "And, talking about Cajun cooking, I'm going to order the crawfish spinach salad, 'lightly breaded crawfish tails on a bed of fresh spinach with slice mushrooms, apple wood smoked bacon, and toasted pecans'. That sounds delicious. I'll ask the waiter which beer he would recommend to go with that."

"So you two have a micro brewery!" said Naomi. "That is remarkable."

"Wow, can't think of a better profession," said Ben.

"It is nice, especially if your beer turns out the way you want, if people really like it and become patrons, but it is a lot of work, believe me," said Will.

"We're a micro brewery or you might also call us a brew-pub because we're a brewery and a restaurant as well. We can't compete with the big breweries by any means, but I think our beer is of better quality and flavor. Craft brewing takes time and we can experiment. People are always coming into our brewery asking us to do this or that," added Meghan.

"You're the brewmaster, Will?" asked Larry.

"No, no, that would be Meghan. I've taken over the restaurant portion of our business and I do all the books. I'm an accountant by profession."

"Wow, Meghan. Sorry. One should never assume. I guess I've made an ass out of myself."

"No sweat. A common mistake. Traditionally, men have always consumed more beer than women, and so it's natural to assume that a brewmaster would be a man. But, studies have shown that women actually consume more of certain types of craft beers."

"I didn't know. What kinds of beer do you brew, Meghan?"

"A variety. Hoppy wheat, lager, porter, IPA, Pilsner. We also offer some fruit beers, currants, apricots, or cranberries. Women like to drink these."

"Sound delicious," said Naomi.

"They are."

***

Once the group had finished dinner, people dispersed. Some stayed by the river, some walked in the park, others made their way to the casino to try their good fortune with lady luck. Justin was sitting alone in a gazebo on a bluff overlooking the Mississippi River. Ryder and Ronny walked up to him and tried to get his attention.

"Mind if we sit with you, Justin?" asked Ryder. There was no response from the tour guide. The two friends walked closer. Justin was staring at the river below them, his mind obviously elsewhere. Once they were closer Ryder asked again. "Is it okay to sit here?"

"Hm?" said Justin, somewhat startled. "Sure. Of course! It's a free country," he responded.

Ryder noticed that Justin had a few tears trickling down his cheeks.

"Are you okay," asked Ryder. "You look a little sad tonight. Miss your family?"

"I don't have any family, but yes, I do miss someone."

"I miss my daughter," said Ryder. "Her mom and I have been divorced for quite a few years now and I only get to see Janie every second weekend. It's not easy. I can only blame myself for that. Even though I was old enough, I was too immature when I got married and just couldn't take the pressure of having a family and a small baby. My daughter was very colicky as a baby, cried all night. I couldn't sleep, I couldn't concentrate at work and so I just left them. I'm a coward plain and simple. I tried to reconnect with my family a few years later because I missed them, but by then it was too late. My wife had already found someone else. I do long for them."

"Ah."

"Do you want to talk about it, Justin?"

"Not really. I miss my wife. She passed away almost a lifetime ago now."

"And you're still mourning her. She must have been very special."

"She was perfect, everything I ever wanted in a woman. But she was taken from me far too early."

"That's so sad," said Ronny. "I have never found the woman of my dreams. I don't think she exists."

"No, you don't understand. My wife was absolutely faultless, the ideal woman."

"Well, no one is perfect, that's what I think," said Ryder. "I was happy with pretty darn good. Of course that didn't work out, but we still talk and we don't say anything negative about our ex-partner in front of our daughter."

"We didn't get a chance to have a family. I wanted to have a lot of children."

"You didn't try to find someone else in all this time?" asked Ronny.

"What are you saying? I could never love or even look at anyone else. That would be a betrayal to my love."

"Wow. To love someone that deeply! That's rare," said Ryder. "I've started dating again, but have to say that it feels weird. I mean, when you've been with someone for any length of time, dating and then married, it's hard to start over."

Justin wiped the tears from his face and stood up. He excused himself and slowly walked back in the direction of the hotel. Ronny and Ryder looked at the back of a very dejected man. "That whole friendliness, that cheerfulness, those smiles in the bus and in the restaurants, they're all forced. He's the saddest man I've ever seen," said Ryder.

"Yeah well, he's got to be friendly. That's his job. Everybody's got to earn a living. I hope he's gonna be all right," added Ronny.

"Did you also notice that he had a little tick? He closed his eyes tightly. I think it happens to people when they get nervous and stressed out."

"Poor guy."

"If he wanted a large family and never got a chance then it was probably a fatal car accident. Maybe he was in the car with her and survived."

"He might feel guilty for surviving. Or it could have been cancer."

"Could have been. In either case, you gotta feel sorry for the guy."

"Yeah."

"By the way, do you have a reefer with you? This is a nice place to chill out."

"As a matter of fact I do. Here."

"Thanks man."

✳✳✳

DARKNESS, it's still my constant companion. It's within me, in my mind and in my heart. And in my soul, my poor fragile soul. This vital force within me will very soon have to sacrifice itself for the most worthy of causes. For there is a light, a glimmer of flickering light that I can see in the distance, a light of hope, joy and ecstasy; a light of justice, retribution and deliverance.

My heart is racing in anticipation of that very special moment. It is pumping the toxic life fluid within me with thrust and fervor. Be loud my heart, keep pumping, keep racing. Be still, my soul, and prepare yourself for your slaughter on the altar. Rejoice, for you are noble in your self-sacrifice, and you will ultimately set me free.

***

Dylan, Brooke, Jordan and Sally found a little bar a few blocks away. Sally and Brooke each ordered a dry martini with an olive. They were deep in conversation.

"I just wonder what kind of mischief my kids are into without proper supervision," said Sally. "My parents were so strict with me when I grew up, but with their grandkids it's a whole different story. 'We're not their parents' they always tell me. 'We are not going to discipline them.' I bet they're staying up way too late watching horror movies and eating chocolate cake before bedtime."

"Why don't you call them," asked Brooke.

"Oh, no. I don't want to spoil what's left of my mini vacation."

"I hear you. My parents are watching Dylan Jr. and they probably offered him a beer. Maybe they're smoking a joint together."

"Your parents smoke weed?"

"I don't know. I don't know at all what they do any more. They're always smiling and laughing, actually way too much."

"Maybe they're reliving their youth, or they're on a second honeymoon of sorts, and..."

"Don't go there please. I don't want to think about it."

"I hear you."

Dylan and Jordan were sitting at the bar enjoying a couple of beers. "Jordan, do you remember the road trip we took with my dad's '57 Chevy all those years ago? When we wanted to impress the chicks we met along the way."

"Do I ever. You wanted to impress some chicks. I had already fallen for Sally and I wasn't interested in anyone else."

"Yeah, well, the trip didn't really turn out the way we wanted. I mean we made it to New Orleans and had some fun on Bourbon Street but then things turned sour. Do you remember?"

"Oh, gawd yes," replied Jordan. "Kind of reminds me of the Albert King lyrics:

Born under a bad sign
Been down since I began to crawl
If it wasn't for bad luck
I wouldn't have no luck at all

"Yeah. We probably shouldn't have gone on that trip at all. What happened in New Orleans haunted me for years. It's still on my mind."

CHAPTER IX

DYLAN AND JORDAN'S BLUES

We're cruisin' in our Chevy
A '57 beaut
We're hoping to pick up chicks
Especially if they're cute
The car I borrowed from my dad
If he knew we're drivin' so far
I'll never get to drive this Chev
Or any other car
That's why I'm blue, of yeah
I've got the cruisin' backroad blues

Rich kid. Poor kid. That was how you could possibly describe Dylan and Jordan. Dylan had many advantages growing up, the most important of which was that his father owned a car dealership in St. Louis. The young child wore expensive clothes. His dad took him to the Cardinals' games, which he loved, and also to watch and listen to the St. Louis Blues, one being a hockey team and the other the piano-based urban style of blues. Dylan was fascinated with music, and who wouldn't be? One of the great rock'n'roll icons who had been influenced early on by the blues was Chuck Berry, a native of St. Louis. Dylan was able to see him perform several times. His father, who loved music as much as his son, took his offspring to Chicago on numerous occasions to listen to the highly amplified music which was based on electric guitar and harmonica.

Dylan joined the school band in grade seven, which at first could not master the kind of music to which he listened. But the squeaks and squeals gave way to organized sound, and after a while, parents attending the year-end concert could find some resemblance to a melody they had once heard. The band was where the young musician met Jordan. Both played in the clarinet section.

When his father passed away, Jordan's mom moved from East St. Louis to become a housekeeper for a well-to-do family across the Mississippi River. She and her son had two rooms at the back of the very large mansion. She was happy for her son, because he was now going to a much better school.

Dylan and Jordan hit it off right away. Dylan, who was a few months older, took Jordan under his wings. Soon they were playing baseball together on the same team, doing homework together, hanging out in the park. They formed a garage band in Dylan's basement with a few of their friends. They let their hair grow long and wore bandanas around their heads, imitating Axl Rose and playing their version of "Sweet Child of Mine". Other artists that appealed to them and that they tried to imitate were Bon Jovi and Springsteen. They tried to come up with their own lyrics. That did not go so well, and after a year or so, the band of great hopes disbanded.

They both attended the same high school, but Jordan knew that his mother would never be able to save enough money to send him to college. When Dylan went to college to pursue a degree in business, his dad offered Jordan an apprenticeship as a mechanic in his dealership. Jordan gratefully accepted the position.

Dylan had finished school and was now working beside his father, learning everything he could, sales, marketing, accounting etc. After a few months of hard work he asked his dad if he and Jordan could have a weekend off. There was a band he wanted to see in Memphis and would it be all right to take one of the cars that his dad proudly owned.

***

"Hey Jordan, did you bring your overnight bag?" asked a curly red-haired young man in his early twenties walking into the automotive center of a car dealership.

"I did," replied a tall, thin and dark-haired man with olive skin. "But you can't be serious. You want to leave right after work?"

"I do," replied Dylan. "We have a lot of miles to cover and not a whole lot of time to do it."

"Yeah, I know, but hey man, drivin' through the night after we've worked all day, isn't that dangerous?"

"Heck no. I had three strong coffees this afternoon and I've packed a whole lot of Cokes and chocolate bars."

"There's a healthy diet. All right, all right, ten more minutes and I'm done. I'll take a quick shower in the back and come out to meet you. So what did you tell your dad?"

"Oh, I just said I'd take our blue and white '57 Chevy for a little ride down to Memphis. Now, there's a car the way it's supposed to look. This car makes a statement."

"So what's it saying?" kidded Jordan.

Dylan turned to his friend with a smile. "You smart ass," he said. "By the way, I told him about a blues band I wanted to see there in some club and that we'd be back on

Sunday night."

"Okay. It's your skin. I mean, we could drive through the night, sleep in a truck stop for a few hours, party on Bourbon Street Saturday night, drive to the same truck stop, get a couple of hours of sleep and head home. Not my kind of fun though."

"Mine neither. When we get to New Orleans I'll call my dad with some made-up mechanical problems and let him know we'll be home a day later. What's he gonna say?"

Friday night at 5:00 pm, Dylan and Jordan began their weekend adventure in the vintage car, tail fins and all. Dangling from the mirror were traditional red, fuzzy dice. Once on the highway, they both felt good and enjoyed the ride.

"Just to let you know, I'm gonna be driving the whole time. This is a very special car and my dad won't let anyone drive it besides him and me."

"That's fine with me. I don't want the responsibility. However, it would be better if we took turns driving, fatigue and all, the drone of the highway."

"I'll be fine. I'm caffeinated and have a lot of adrenaline. And a lot of fear. If my dad finds out he's going to kill me."

"He'll be upset all right."

This being February, darkness set in very early. The roads had been plowed after the last heavy snowfall, but there were a lot of large trucks on the road driving a lot faster than the Chevy. After several hours of driving, Jordan nudged his partner.

"Hey Dylan," he said.

"What?"

"My stomach is growling. We left right after work and

have been driving for five hours. How about stopping for a quick bite to eat?"

"Sounds good. I'll gas up and we can go for a burger."

An hour's drive south of Memphis, Dylan drove into a quaint little restaurant which had a gas bar and motel in the back. He pumped gas into the tank while Jordan cleaned the windshield of all the slush that had caked onto it. Both walked into the small restaurant. He paid for the gas and notified the waitress walking by that he and his buddy would like to order a burger, fries and a Coke and quickly. They were in a hurry. He noticed two young women sitting at a table. He walked over to them and plunked himself down and motioned to Jordan to do the same.

The girls, totally flabbergasted by the bold action, couldn't get out the words "buzz off" like they wanted to.

"Hi, my name is Dylan and this is my friend Jordan. We're from St. Louis and on our way to Mardi Gras. How about you?" he asked, looking at the girls.

There was a short pause in a reply. "Mhm, I'm Rachel and this is my best friend Ruth. We're from Erie, Pennsylvania."

"Eerie, sounds ominous. You're on a road trip?"

"I guess so. We stayed in Louisville, Kentucky, overnight. Today, we did a tour of the National Civil Rights Museum, the old Lorraine Motel. We walked an hour or so on Beale Street and bought a couple of jazz CDs. Thereafter we left Memphis and drove a bit further to this motel. And here we are."

"Headed south, I gather."

"To New Orleans, like you," said Ruth. Rachel gave her a kick under the table.

"Where you staying down there?" asked Dylan.

"We haven't booked a hotel yet. We're not sure that our

old car can make it all the way."

"Well, in that case, here is the name of the hotel where we're staying. It's in the French Quarter. If all the hotels are full, you can stay with us. I booked a room with two double beds."

"Thank you," said Ruth.

Jordan and Dylan were served very quickly, inhaled their meals, and in a flash they were gone.

"Why didn't you give them our real names?" asked Ruth.

"Because I don't like Dylan. I don't go for macho brag-garts. 'My father owns a car dealership. I drive a '57 Chevy.' Me, me, me, me."

"I kind of liked Jordan, although who knows what he's like. He never had a chance to get a word in edgewise."

"I hope we never see them again."

"Never say never! He was right. All the hotels might be occupied. We may have to take them up on their offer."

"Heaven help us! I will set down the rules right away," said Rachel.

"You will. We've been in youth hostels in Europe. Wouldn't be any different."

"Please don't ever do that again," said Jordan.

"Do what?" asked Dylan.

"Come on like that to girls you don't even know. I was uncomfortable during the whole meal and the girls were definitely not interested in us."

"That's their loss."

"Get off your high horse. I told you I'm not interested in picking up girls. I've got Sally."

"Mustang Sally!"

"Don't call her that."

"I wouldn't be surprised if we saw those two eerie girls again. I'll bet all the hotel rooms are taken."

"We'll see."

***

It was getting near midnight. Jordan's eyes kept closing, but he tried to stay awake to be sure that his driver was as well. The car radio was tuned in to a rock station, fittingly playing "Enter Sandman." Jordan was humming along:

Sleep with one eye open
Gripping your pillow tight
Exit light
Enter night
Take my hand
We're off to never never land.

Suddenly, Jordan saw headlights coming straight towards them. He blinked his eyes to make sure he wasn't just dreaming and shouted to Dylan. He had seen the strange headlights as well and swerved onto the shoulder of the road. Immediately, a car passed them.

"Did you see that? What an idiot. He's driving on the wrong side of the freeway. How is that even possible?"

"Oh my gawd, we're lucky to be alive," said Jordan. "A ghost driver! He must be drunk and entered the interstate on the wrong ramp."

"If he continues, he'll kill someone and himself with a head-on collision."

"What should we do?"

"I don't know. Get off on the next ramp and we'll take

a breather."

Dylan drove his car off the next exit and found a place to rest at the side of the road.

"I don't know about you, man," said Jordan. "Maybe we should turn around and go home, or just back to Memphis. It's not that far. Maybe this was a sign or something."

"And maybe you've got too much of an imagination," said Dylan. "Nope, we've got the time and we've got the car to impress a few chicks. We're gonna get to Mardi Gras come hell or high water."

"If that's what you want. I could use a drink."

"Help yourself. There's some beer in the backseat cooler."

"You want some?"

"Nope. I'm driving, gotta keep my head clear. And just to let you know. After that near mishap, I'm now fully awake, so I can keep on driving."

Chapter X

New Orleans – The Big Easy, Birthplace of Jazz

It was the third day of this magnificent trip. People slowly congregated in the hotel's restaurant for breakfast. Some were bright-eyed and alert and others, one could tell, had stayed up far into the night, a few at the casino and others at local bars. Justin and Mike were already getting things ready on the bus.

"Good morning folks. Hope you enjoyed your evening in Natchez. I know I did," said Justin.

"Nice weather we're having, eh?" said Big Mike as Meghan and Will were boarding the bus. They looked at him in surprise.

"Are you Canadian?" Meghan asked the bus driver.

"No, no. I just heard that you guys were. You and that other couple."

"Ah. Yes, we are."

Justin gave a dirty look to Mike but then caught himself, put on a big smile and continued addressing the passengers. "We are now on the final leg of our great journey, the end destination, New Orleans. It's going to take us about three hours to get there. People call it the Big Easy, The Cradle of Jazz. It is like no other city that I know. It is truly amazing."

Once in The Big Easy, the group would be split up. Justin informed his passengers that it was impossible to have everyone at the same hotel and still be in the French Quarter. They would all be staying in smaller hotels. Each one would be within walking distance of Bourbon Street, and also of quaint little restaurants and specialty shops. Each hotel he had picked would be clean and comfortable and have that old-world charm but new-world luxury.

"After you check in, you'll be free to do whatever. You can go to Bourbon Street and walk up and down the road with a Hurricane in your hand. It's delicious, a lot of rum, syrup and juices. Preservation Hall should not be missed. It's small so sometimes you might have to stand outside, but that's okay. You'll still be able to hear the beautiful music. Just don't ask them to play 'When the Saints Go Marching in.' They have played that song a million times, but if you insist, you'll have to fork over some real cash.

"Some of you might want to walk down to the harbor and have some real Creole food, hot and spicy. Crawfish is a real treat. I have booked a pretty swanky restaurant for dinner tonight. Since this is our last night together as a group, it would be great to wine and dine and then afterwards, go to a blues club together. Some of you will be flying home tomorrow. I'm sure you'll be having mixed feelings about that. Others are here on an extended stay. We'll say our good-byes this evening. We'll all meet outside the restaurant at 7:00 pm. I'm going to give you the name and address in a minute."

***

"We'll be in the birthplace of jazz today! I'm so excited!" said Larry. "You know, one of my all-time favorite movies is *Chicago*. Renée Zellweger and Catherine Zeta-Jones, they were hot."

"Well, Richard Gere and Taye Diggs weren't so bad-looking either, you know. Real eye candy," said Hannah.

"You think so?"

"Yeah. Do you still remember some of the lines?"

"Let me think. Here goes."

Larry: *Come on babe*
   Why don't we paint the town?
Hannah: *And all that Jazz*
L: Da, da, da,
   Da, da, da, da, da, da
H: *And all that Jazz*
L: *Start the car*
   I know a whoopee spot
   Where the gin is cold
   But the piano's hot
H: Da, da, da, and so on and on
Both: *And all*, da, da, da, da, da,
   That
   Da da da da da
   Jazz, da da da da da
   Yeah!

"We're going to have to work on that," Hannah said with a smile.

***

The bus was entering Baton Rouge. The traffic was very heavy and the bus inched its way forward and had come to a complete stop. Jim, looking out the window, wondered what could be causing the gridlock. He tapped the person sitting directly in front of him on the shoulder.

"Do you know why we're in such heavy traffic?" he asked.

"Oh, I think we're very close to the A.W. Mumford Stadium. Today must be a college football game."

"This many people come to watch a college football game?"

"Gawd, yes. College football is almost as big as the NFL. Do you watch football up in Canada?" asked Ryder.

"I guess some people do," said Jim.

"No, no, it's ice hockey, am I right?"

"I suppose, they're always saying it's our national sport, but I think it's actually lacrosse."

"Is that a game? Never heard of it."

"Our family members are actually all soccer fanatics. My uncle ran a whole minor league consisting of twelve teams. My mom and aunt voluntarily ran a concession booth to make money for minor league soccer. Both my sister and brother played, coached and refereed soccer matches."

"Wow. But that's only in the Canadian summer. What do you do the other ten months of the year? Watch snowflakes fall?"

"Exactly. We're mesmerized by falling snow. I mean, every snowflake is different from the other. Billions of flakes. It's mind-boggling."

"Gotta keep yourself occupied in those long, long winter months, I imagine."

"Well, I chop wood all winter for the stove in our cabin.

I go ice-fishing. You know, drill a hole through the ice and catch frozen fish. We used to skate but now we ride snow-mobiles to take the kids to school. I drive a snow plow to keep the roads open for those ten months and Sarah sews quilts for our beds and knits socks for me and the kids."

"That's a hard life. How did you hear about this trip way down here?"

"Oh, that, yeah. We always put a couple of coat hangers on the antenna of our radio. On really crisp and clear nights, when you can see the Milky Way, you know, millions of stars, we get really good reception. Sometimes a station in Nashville comes in and we listen to country music. Other nights we get Memphis and then we listen to the blues. That's how we heard about the contest. We entered and won this trip."

"Wow, you won this trip too?"

"Yup. Really excited to catch some rays, listen to good music and enjoy southern cooking."

"You must be looking forward to a steak dinner this evening."

"To be honest, up in Canada, we eat mostly game meat, moose, deer, ducks. Actually, I'm a bit apprehensive about eating pork, chicken or beef. But fish, now that's a whole different ballgame. Can't wait to have some catfish in New Orleans."

"Do you have to do that?" Sarah asked her husband after Ryder had turned around.

"Do what?" asked Jim.

"Pull people's legs like that?"

"He is a bit short at one end. Hah, hah. He started with the ten-month winter in Canada. I just carried it a bit further."

"Groan. He's from California, you know, Land of Eternal Sunshine. What could he possibly know about Canada?"

"He should know something, other than the fact that it snows in Canada."

"You think we're that important?"

"Well, aren't we?"

"All right, wise guy, what do you know about California?"

"Well, there's Disneyland as opposed to Disneyworld, which is in Florida."

"Aha."

"And there's Hollywood. Ah, and they grow a lot of grapes."

"That's it? That's all you know?"

"What else could there be?"

"Think I made my point. Also, he didn't actually believe you, you know. He winked at me before turning around."

✳✳✳

Meghan and Will were very excited in anticipation of spending a few days in the Cajun capital. They were going through some of the brochures they had downloaded back home and then printed.

"I can't decide what to do first," said Meghan. "There are several tours in the French Quarter where we can do some food sampling. One stops by some really great restaurants where we can sample seafood gumbo, Creole biscuits and beignets. Another tour stops at Creole eateries, artisanal shops and markets where we can again sample gumbo, po' boys and pralines."

"And here," said Will, "we can go to a cooking demonstration of gumbo, jambalaya and sample them with local beer. We shouldn't miss this one."

"You know, why don't we do all three? Let's extend our vacation for a couple more days and rebook our flight back home."

"Sounds good to me. What about Jim and Sarah, do you think they'll want to stay longer?"

"Let's ask them."

***

Sally was looking at a travel guide she had picked up at her local AAA.

"Jordan, let's plan our next two days. We can't do a whole lot today because we have the farewell dinner with the entire group tonight. As soon as we're settled into our hotel let's see if we can get a last-minute booking of the three-hour bus tour. We'll get a tour through the French Quarter where they'll highlight the most interesting places, drive through the Garden District where we'll see those beautiful antebellum mansions with the Greek revival architecture. We'll also pass the lakefront where the levies were breached by Hurricane Katrina."

"That sounds like something I'd like to see. Those poor people living in Katrina's path. Tomorrow I also want to go on that full-day swamp and plantation tour. I want to see some alligators in the bayous of the cypress swamps."

"Well, maybe you and Dylan could do that while Brooke and I go on that paddle wheeler, the Natchez. It's supposed to be the last original one, you know. There'll be great music, great scenery and a luncheon. I think that's more up my alley."

"All right then, we'll ask them."

***

The bus arrived in New Orleans in the early afternoon. This, the final destination, was the highlight of the entire trip. Other places they had visited were great, but for jazz and blues lovers, this city was the epicenter. Small groups of passengers were dispersed to quaint little hotels. One of the inns was a Victorian house surrounded by an iron fence that looked like cornstalks. In the lobby, crystal chandeliers reflected ornate mirrors. The rooms were stuffed with antique furniture and had stained-glass windows and canopy beds. Comfort at its finest.

Mike took out the luggage and placed it on the sidewalk, keeping his head down, not once looking at his passengers.

"Is he antisocial, or just too shy to say anything to us?" wondered Sally.

"Maybe he's got tears in his eyes and doesn't want us to see that, because he's gonna miss us so much," said Brooke.

"Yeah, right," said Dylan. "After three days on the road he's made an unbreakable bond with us."

"Do you always have to be like that?" said his wife.

"Like what?"

"So sarcastic."

***

Upon leaving their hotel, Ryder and Ronny headed straight to Bourbon Street and bought themselves a Hurricane drink. They were bumping their way through the throngs of people who were walking in the center of the street, trying not to spill their precious beverages.

"We should get a snack of some sort. Dinner won't be for a few hours yet."

"Let's go for some Jambalaya. How hot do you like it?" asked Ryder.

"Well, I don't want it too hot going in, and out the next day, if you know what I mean."

"Oh, I do. I remember very well the last time we were here. So not very spicy for both of us."

"Hey Ryder, we're staying one more night after tonight. Are you game with going on one of those walking tours, you know, voodoo, vampire, ghost tour? They take you past these haunted houses and then to the creepiest graveyard on earth. Nobody's buried in this city, you know, because of the high water level. That in itself is pretty spooky," said Ronny.

"I'll think about it. I'll let you know tomorrow."

"I guess that means no."

"No, but it doesn't mean yes either."

"Hey, aren't those our Pittsburghers standing in front of that old rustic building?"

"You make it sound like a new choice in hamburgers."

"Yeah, this one is made of squirrel meat."

"What?!"

"I'm kidding. That's a joke, man. They're from Squirrel Hill, Pittsburgh."

"I didn't know that and I'm not gonna forget it either."

"Hey, Hannah!" Ronny yelled. "Wait up before you go inside!"

When they had caught up with Hannah, Naomi and their

spouses, Ronny said: "We should go into Preservation Hall together. After all, this is the eye of the Jazz Hurricane."

"Wow, you're full of it today," said Ryder.

"Sure, join us," said Hannah. "We can hear the band out here, but I want to see them. This is kind of a high point for us for this trip."

Once inside, the six music enthusiasts stood behind people sitting on worn benches, which complemented the wooden floors and walls where the plaster was crumbling. None of this mattered. It was the music they had come to hear. After the set, they decided to go to the Jazz Museum. They would be going to a blues club in the evening. Everything had to be condensed into as little time as possible. The two couples from Pittsburgh had decided to stay a few days extra and would be looking for a popular jazz club the following evening as the highlight of their excursion.

***

Justin had booked a section of a well-known restaurant for his passengers, Big Mike and himself. The mirrors on the walls reflected the light of the crystal chandeliers. Tables of four were covered with white tablecloths.

The menu was very diverse, from duck and andouille gumbo soup to a bouillabaisse, a hearty soup popular in Marseilles, France.

Jordan and Sally saw an elderly couple, cohorts on their adventure, sitting alone at a table meant for four.

"May we join you?" asked Sally.

"Oh, please do, luv," said the elderly lady. "You usually sit with that other couple, I think their names are Dylan and Brooke."

"Yes, yes. We're actually very good friends, but everyone needs a little time and space."

"I suppose."

"Dylan hasn't been in the greatest of moods because Brooke is always reprimanding him that he drinks too much. He always insists that he is on a well-deserved holiday and she should leave him alone," said Jordan.

Over the years, his friend had become moody and miserable. Dylan and his father had given him everything, first a trade and then a fantastic career as manager of the automotive center. He owed them everything. Even so, he felt that he had an albatross around his neck. Work was one thing, but socializing with Dylan and Brooke had become more of an obligation. Jordan felt gagged, he felt guilty.

"Brooke keeps on babbling," added Sally.

"That's very funny," said the elderly lady. "And I've noticed on the bus that she has this annoying hysterical laugh that sounds like a possessed sewing machine. It's very fortunate though that she doesn't really laugh all that much."

Are you from England, your accent and all?" asked Jordan.

"Why yes, dearie. We're from Liverpool. And you?"

"St. Louis," replied Sally.

"Ah, the city with the big arch."

"Yup, gateway to the West. So how did you get to be on this bus tour?"

"Well, we were looking at doing something different and our travel agent showed us this. Oddly enough, our agent had never heard of this tour company before, but the tour sounded so good. And we are music lovers."

"We did take out cancellation insurance, of course, in

case this was all bogus, but look, here we are and this is a great tour," said her husband.

"And our tour guide is so knowledgeable and friendly to boot," added his wife. "Yes, we've really enjoyed this trip so far."

Just then Dylan and Brooke walked past the table and gave their friends a dirty look. Jordan raised his shoulder and pointed to all the tables full of people. He also pointed to the far corner of the restaurant where there were a few empty seats.

The waitress brought everyone the menu. "Your sommelier will be with you in a minute," she said.

"A sommelier, wow. Very classy," said Sally.

"Look at this menu, jumbo lump crab in a variety of ways," said the English lady.

"Fish, for me. I'm not into shellfish. I know what salmon is but what is a lemon fish or a redfish or black drum?" asked her husband.

"No clue. Ask the waitress."

"Filet mignon sounds good," said Jordan.

"I'm going to try the bouillabaisse," Sally decided.

***

After everyone had placed their orders, Justin stood up and spoke to the group. "After dinner, a local tour guide will take most of you to a really great blues club. For the people who were online winners of this tour, there is a little surprise for them. Mike and I will take them someplace very special. It won't take more than an hour or so and then we'll all join you at the club so that we can have our last few hours of this tour together. I have to say it has been a very positive experience for me. You've all been great. I want to thank each and every one of you for making this easy for Mike and myself. It's been a real pleasure to work for you. Perhaps we'll see you again on this or another tour."

CHAPTER XI

THE TOMBSTONE

The eight online winners and their spouses boarded the bus wondering where they were headed. Once aboard, Justin, with the help of Mike, poured champagne into flutes and handed them to all aboard. "Don't be shy. There's plenty of champagne and you don't have to have only one glass," he said.

"This is great, Justin," said Meghan.

"I still can't believe that we won such a great tour and not just the bus ride but everything else we have experienced. Who financed all of this? None of us were ever able to figure this out. I mean, it's quite a bit of money," said Will.

"Oh don't you worry too much about that. I will tell you in due time, but first enjoy the champagne," said the tour guide.

"Aren't you going to have any?" asked Sarah.

"Well, technically I'm still on duty, so to speak, and Mike is driving, so no. It's just water or a pop for us, although I could go for a double-double right about now."

"A what?" asked Dylan.

"It's a Tim Hortons coffee with two creams and two sugars. Everyone in Canada knows what a double-double is," said Jim. "Are you Canadian, Justin?"

"I've been there."

"I don't know how many drinks I've had today but I'm

beginning to feel a little woozy right now," said Ryder.

"So am I," said Ronny.

One by one the passengers slumped into their seats. Justin looked at his passengers and smirked. Once they had all fallen asleep, he took a syringe and injected a liquid night-time sleep aid into Jim, Will, Ben, Larry, Brooke and Sally.

"Sleepy, sleepy time my sweets," he said. "Enjoy a few hours in never-never land. I'm being so nice to you. You won't even be that groggy in the morning."

"That's actually a lie," said Big Mike. "They'll all have massive headaches tomorrow morning."

"My heart bleeds for them," Justin said sarcastically.

Mike started the ignition of the bus. He put a CD of Justin's favorite songs into the CD player. The first song on his playlist was Falco's "Out of the Dark".

Your hell burns inside of me
You're my elixir to survive

...

Do I have to die
In order to live

He drove several blocks until he got to a cemetery. He stopped the bus. It was already dark, but there was light from an almost full moon. One by one, Mike and Justin carried Meghan, Sarah, Naomi, Hannah, Dylan, Jordan, Ryder and Ronny into a large tomb within the cemetery. Mike returned to the bus and drove it a few hundred feet forward so that it would be somewhat hidden under some large, dark trees. He walked back to the cemetery.

***

Ryder was the first to wake up, but very slowly. He was completely confused and disorientated. He was in a very dark, damp and musty-smelling room. There was another smell, that of vanilla-scented burning candles. It couldn't be his hotel room, he reasoned. He took in more of the room as his eyes became adjusted to the darkness. He heard some rustling all around him.

"Where am I?" asked Ryder, still half asleep, and struggling to free himself.

"Why are my hands tied behind my back?" asked Dylan, now waking up.

"Wakee, wakee, my little lambs. It's almost time for the slaughter," said Justin. One by one his captives awoke.

A large stone casket was situated in the center of a very dark room. Candles were burning on ledges all around the sarcophagus, giving off enough light for Dylan to notice others who were sitting on a cement floor, leaning against dank walls. The bus driver and tour guide were sitting on stone steps leading down into the interior of a tomb, each holding a lantern in their hand. Other prisoners were beginning to wake up.

"Where am I?" asked Meghan. "It's so dark in here I can't see very much. Will, where are you?"

"Not in here," replied Justin, his eyes cold as ice.

Jordan, waking up, looked around at the others. "Where is my wife?" he asked.

"Oh, she's safe, along with the others, and sound and ever sooo sleepy back on the bus. The rest of you are here in the cemetery. You remember this cemetery, don't you?

We were all here twenty-five years ago, outside this very tomb, stoned out of our minds."

"What are you talking about?" said Sarah. "I've never been stoned."

"Oh, I think you were, but don't want to admit it. You've put the ugly incident so far into the back of your mind that you don't remember, but it will come back to you very soon. I'll make sure of that."

"I've never been in a cemetery in New Orleans," objected Ronny, who had just awakened with a splitting headache.

"Oh, you have, Ronny, you and Ryder. You rode here on your Honda Shadows and stayed at the same dumpy hotel like the rest of us. That's where we all met, in the dining room."

"Who are you? Really? How do you know what we were driving?" asked Ronny.

"My name, of course, is not Justin, although that's apropos, isn't it. After all, I want justice. No, my real name is Jonathan. I'm not omniscient, but I know a lot."

"Are you equating yourself with God?" asked Dylan.

"*Au contraire*, Dylan, *au contraire*. But God does say in Romans 1:18 'For the wrath of God is revealed from heaven against all ungodliness and unrighteousness of men, who by their unrighteousness suppress the truth.'"

"You can quote the Bible? What are you, some kind of religious fanatic?" asked Sarah.

"I think it's safe to say that you can keep the 'religious' out of that equation," Jonathan said using air quotes when he said 'religious.' Turning to Dylan, he said: "Back to what's really important. You and Jordan were here as well, easing on down the road in your '57 Chevrolet, quite a classic car. Hard to forget."

"Wow, you know a lot about us."

"Yes, and you ladies, Meghan and Sarah, you sputtered into the Big Easy in your old, beat up Volkswagen Camper, two malodorous, disheveled latter-day hippies. Easy to remember."

"We didn't smell that bad, and we took a shower as often as we could."

"How very considerate of all the other guests in the hotel. And you two, Naomi and Hannah, you inched yourselves down highways and secondary roads in your '68 Volkswagen Beetle. Another one of those vintage cars, but not as classy as a '57 Chevy."

"How do you know all this? And why are we here?" asked Naomi.

Jonathan turned on a flashlight and illuminated a picture that he had hung on one of the walls inside the tomb.

"Does that bring back any memories? Yes? No?" He took the picture from the wall and showed it to all his captives. The lantern he was carrying illuminated his twisted, almost ghoulish-looking face.

"She looks somewhat familiar," said Meghan.

"Of course she does," he said, his eyes burning with hatred. "That's Margie, my angel, my love, my everything. She was the perfect woman. Too soon was she taken from me. We were just married and on our honeymoon."

Chapter XII

Jonathan and Margie's Blues

We're crossing now the border
Pacific to our right
Embarking on our honeymoon
To see the West Coast sights
We're young and poor but happy
The world is at our feet
We smile and we are friendly
With all those that we meet
We are not blue, oh no
We have no traveling backroad blues

Jonathan, a tall man with short dark hair and sunken eyes, had attended a week-long church retreat in a camp in a forest north of Vancouver, British Columbia. He ventured alone along a trail and got lost. After four days of wandering in the wilderness without food or water, he heard a voice. A counselor who knew the area well eventually found him said: "Follow me. I know the way back to the camp." All Jonathan heard in his state of dehydration and delirium was: "Follow me." He believed it to be the voice of God. After speaking with his minister who believed this was a great opportunity for recruitment because the flock was far greater than the number of shepherds able to lead them, told the young man that this was nothing less than a miracle. God had spoken to Jonathan. There was only one thing that could be done. The young man was encouraged to enroll in a four-year Master of Divinity program at a Bible College with the intent of becoming an ordained minister.

He took courses in theology, religious heritage, biblical studies, church ministry, leadership, pastoral care of the dying and their families who were grieving after the loss of their loved one. He learned about Christianity and the secular culture all around him. He began to have a deepening faith and it showed in his devout life. He became the personification, the embodiment, of a true Christian. He shared the church doctrine with others. He would preach and teach.

He had finished his four years of studies and was now in his one year of internship. During the Sunday services, the young vicar read the Old Testament readings, the epistles and, twice monthly, helped with the distribution of wafers and wine, the body and blood of the Lord, during the holy communion.

He visited the sick and the dying in hospitals, palliative care facilities and retirement homes, bringing the suffering the word of God and giving them peace and hope. It was during one of these visits that he saw her, an angel sent to him from above.

Margie, a five-foot-ten blonde with beautiful blue eyes, worked as a nurse in a retirement home. She cared for and empathized with her ailing patients. They had had a short conversation and realized they belonged to the same congregation. From that moment on she began to attend church services regularly, always sitting in one of the back pews with her parents.

Jonathan summoned his courage as she was walking out

of the nave. He was standing at the door shaking hands and wishing the parishioners a blessed week. Margie noticed that his hands were especially soft and his fingernails well-manicured. He asked her if she would be willing to help with the Christmas Bazaar this year. She, of course, worked full time and she did not have time to set up, knit or bake, something she didn't know how to do anyways, but she told him that she could be there the five hours of the bazaar. When she arrived one half-hour before the door opened to the public, she was told she would be serving coffee and cake from nine until eleven o'clock and then soup and a bun, along with the dessert and a beverage thereafter. Jonathan, as fate would have it, or more likely, upon his request, stood alongside Margie taking orders, serving and removing used dishes and cutlery. He was in heaven.

The young man from then on asked his favorite parishioner to every church function or social that he could think of. One being the choir practices, his voice a deep and full baritone. Margie's voice was not as strong but she never sang out of tune and complemented the others with her lovely alto.

After a year and the end of Jonathan's vicarage, the two were married. It was a lovely wedding attended by the entire congregation. Jonathan had had a call to become the minister of a small congregation in Ontario. Before heading East with his lovely bride, Jonathan and Margie decided to spend their honeymoon driving along the Pacific Coast from Vancouver all the way to San Diego. They would then head diagonally through the States and make their way up to Ontario. Hanging from their rear-view mirror was a stained glass crucifix. Jonathan wanted to be sure he and Margie would be protected from road mishaps caused by careless drivers or intense storms.

On their journey, Jonathan thanked God for the gift of his lovely bride. Both gave thanks for the food they ate, for the beautiful sunsets they saw over the Pacific, for the magnificent redwood forests, some trees over a thousand years old standing upright and strong as the couple's church. And although neither one was a regular drinker of alcoholic beverages, they did buy and drink some wine in Napa Valley. After all, Jesus had made water into wine at the Wedding at Cana, so wine was quite all right.

They had agreed upon a route once they got to San Diego, but Jonathan quite suddenly tried to persuade Margie to change the course. It was February and would it not be grand to take the "Burban," a name they'd given their vehicle, to Bourbon Street in New Orleans.

"New Orleans? You want to go there?" asked Margie, quite taken aback.

"Why not? It will be Mardi Gras when we get there," responded her husband.

"But Jonathan, it's a den of iniquity. People get inebriated and do all sorts of other non-Christian things."

"Well, so maybe we'll be the missionaries and do good in a jungle of wickedness," replied the minister.

"You want to proclaim the Word to some drunks in the French Quarter?"

"No, I just want to enjoy a few days of fun and amusement before we head north to our new congregation. Once we're there, it will mostly be stern faces and I will be watched and judged, as will you, my honeybun."

"Honeybun?"

"It's a term of endearment."

"I think the last time that term was used was two hundred years ago, shnookums."

"Shnookums, eh! Yikes. Okay, okay. I take honeybun back."

"I'm not so sure about this. Last night, I had a strange dream about people with horrible-looking masks on. They were surrounding me and I could hardly breathe, Jonathan. Do you think it's a sign?"

"I think we had too much pizza yesterday. I've had nightmares like that before when I've eaten too late in the evening. Don't think anything of it."

Margie was not completely convinced by her husband's interpretation of her dream, but wanted to please him, so she agreed to go. "All right then, let's go for the great food."

"The great music."

"A ride on a riverboat."

"A colorful parade."

"I'm actually not that crazy about going to New Orleans. However, now that I've made a compromise, I would like you to meet me half way with something too."

"What is it?"

"As I said to you before we left for our honeymoon, once we get to Ontario I want to continue my profession as a nurse. At least let me work on a part-time basis. I spent all those years in nursing school and then working in the retirement home. I really like my profession."

"I don't know if you'll have time, Margie, the congregation will expect you to lead some of the women's groups, prayer meetings, sewing blankets for third-world countries, working in the church kitchen and serving in the basement at special church dinners."

"Jonathan, I can't sew, and when there are too many

people around me, I get nervous."

"Don't panic, sweets. It will be fine. We're going to start a family soon and that will most certainly keep you busy at home, like a good little wife. I hope we have at least a half-dozen children. Don't fret, my love, I will be the shepherd and you will be..."

"Your sheep dog?"

"No, of course not. My helper."

Margie looked at her husband. Why had they not discussed any of this in greater detail? New Orleans sounded really good. Never mind being missionaries in a den of iniquity. A few Hurricane drinks on Bourbon Street and perhaps something stronger is what she needed right about now.

Chapter XIII

City of the Dead – A New Orleans Graveyard

Jonathan's eyes were misty. His voice cracked every time he mentioned his wife's name, as he told the story of his honeymoon. He had spent far too little time with his beloved. His sunken eyes turned to fire as he turned and glanced at all those held captive in the tomb.

"We came to New Orleans and met all of you at that God-forsaken hotel and then, young and stupid as we were, drunk from all those drinks on Bourbon Street and walked to this very cemetery, and that is where Margie was murdered. And one of you is the murderer. We are here tonight, and one of you is going to confess and then suffer the consequences."

"You're mad!" Meghan cried out loud.

"That's right. I'm a crazy Canuck, I admit it," said her captor.

"None of us are murderers. Yes, we were in New Orleans. It's all coming back to me. We walked around Bourbon Street, had a lot to drink and then went for a long walk ending in a cemetery," said Ryder.

"Right, we smoked some weed, some had a mickey and we sat here and looked at the full moon. Someone actually howled at the moon. I remember that," added Ronny.

"You know I'm surprised that none of you recognized

each other," said Jonathan

The eight captives were thinking hard and long why they hadn't recognized each other on their three-day trip. But to be fair, twenty five years had passed and they had all changed in one form or another. People had gained weight, as was the case for Jordan. He had put on forty pounds because of Sally's good cooking. Some had lost weight, one can't actually say baby fat because they were all in their early twenties back then. Some replaced their contact lenses with glasses and vice versa, whatever worked best for them. Others had changed the color of their hair, or simply stopped dying it perhaps to look more professional with the onset of gray streaks. Clothes as well were a big thing. Some, like Sarah, who looked like a latter-day hippie during her camper trip with Meghan was now wearing very smart-looking threads. Others had expensive and comfortable travel-appropriate clothing. Dylan was now over-compensating his loss of hair on his head with facial hair. Ronny's long hair was now cropped short.

They had met at the motel late in the afternoon and had only spent a few hours together. By the time they reached Bourbon Street darkness had already set in. Most of them had far too much to drink back then and besides the alcohol, some had smoked weed and others swallowed some pretty potent drugs. Jordan did not pay attention to the others back then. He was only thinking of Sally and hoping to soon be in the back of the very tight red Daytona with the windshields all steamed up.

Meghan had been the only one to recognize one of the fellow passengers, Dylan. She had noticed that his eyes were of different colors, one gray-green and the other gray-blue.

Not that noticeable, really. If one had been blue and the other brown, surely most people would have noticed this. Of course, he mostly wore tinted glasses and so his heterochromia was hidden. Meghan had mentioned this to her friend Sarah, but her friend had never noticed Dylan's eyes. Twenty-five years ago, she had visions in her head. It wasn't Christmas so it wasn't visions of sugar plums dancing in her head, but fluffy and puffy donuts, sweet and round, cream-filled and chocolate-covered, some of which were glazed, also a good description if one had looked into Sarah's eyes at that moment. With no support from her friend, Meghan had dropped the subject and so didn't put two and two together. Perhaps she would have confronted Jonathan long before and could have averted this dreadful reunion in the cemetery.

Jonathan walked over to where Ronny and Ryder were sitting uncomfortably on the damp cement floor.

"You two are from Orange County in California, surely you've come across drugs. It's famous for them. You brought them here to the cemetery. I remember the decal on your bike, Ryder, that of your comic hero 'The Shadow.' 'Who knows what evil lurks in the hearts of men? The Shadow knows!' As a matter of fact, I am the Shadow, actually only a shadow of my former self, yet still my knowledge surpasses infinity. You and Ronny killed my Margie. You are both evil."

"That's not true!" protested Ryder.

"We only smoked one or two joints, not hard stuff. We were driving motorcycles, had to keep our minds focused on the road. We couldn't overdo it," said Ronny.

"How do you know we're from Orange County?" asked Ryder.

"I'll get to that," replied their captor.

"And you, Sarah, you and your girlfriend Meghan are from Niagara. You were on a long trip through the States. Surely you had something to keep you entertained along the long boring drive on the paved and gravel roads."

"We were just out of school and didn't have a penny to our names. And, we couldn't have anything in the camper. Could have been searched crossing the border into the States," countered Sarah.

"All we did is share a mickey of rum that night. I remember. No drugs," added Meghan.

Justin walked over to Naomi and Hannah.

"Two good girls from Squirrel Hill, Pittsburgh. But good girls are really bad sometimes. What did you bring to this cemetery?"

"Nothing! Ryder gave us each a reefer. That's all we had. We didn't give anything to anybody. Honest," pleaded Naomi.

Justin now walked over to Jordan and Dylan.

"Dylan, your father owns a car dealership. Surely you had a lot of money, driving your daddy's car, trying to impress the ladies. Be honest."

"All right. Yes, Jordan and I had a couple of reefers, but that's it. We didn't offer them to anyone else. How do you know where I come from?"

"Oh, that's easy. I've been trying to find the eight of you for a very long time, ever since Margie was brutally murdered here in the cemetery. After the funeral, I couldn't cope with life anymore and I took my Suburban, the one we had been driving on our honeymoon, and I drove to a cabin deep in the woods of British Columbia. I stayed there for years, foraging for food in the forest, digging for mushrooms. And all I could ever think of was my love and the eight people who had taken her away from me.

"I finally came out of the woods and decided to find you. My mind became clear and focused after a near-death experience. I had one thing, and only one thing, in mind: to find all eight of you and find the murderer, find justice and peace in that and within me. Dylan and Jordan were the easiest to find. I mean, who has a '57 Chevy and whose father owns a car dealership in St. Louis? Didn't take long.

"Ryder and Ronny took a little longer. I mean, who gives up a classic Honda Shadow, and once a motorcycle rider, always a motorcycle rider. I knew you came from Orange County and I remembered partial plate numbers. I got in touch with a shady gumshoe who had contacts in the police department and he found the both of you. You're both driving newer less powerful machines now, but you kept your first bikes in the garage, only taking them out for a little spin now and then.

"Hannah and Naomi took very little time. I remembered that you said you were from Squirrel Hill in Pittsburgh. It wasn't that hard to find VW Beetle repair shops, I asked a few questions and I had you. You probably still have that old Beetle and take it out for a spin in the summer.

"Had to go to Niagara, to find you two. Again, a VW repair shop, there aren't that many, a few questions, and there I got Meghan and Sarah and their adventures in a VW camper. It was still the talk of the mechanic, after all those years."

"How did you get us all together on this trip?" asked Meghan.

"It took some doing. I've been stalking all of you on Facebook for years. I became one of your friends, a long-forgotten friend from high school. I looked through yearbooks, at your class lists and pretended to be one of your old school mates. We've all had great online chats.

"I hired the services of a programmer. Each one of you was enticed in participating in an online contest. I matched the contest to your individual tastes. Dylan was the easiest. He really likes the blues, played them in a band in high school, went to blues clubs in St. Louis, took his wife and friends to listen to some Chicago Blues in the Windy City.

"Hannah and Naomi actually like jazz better, so I really pitched the jazz clubs we would stop in along the route, especially in New Orleans. It was a cinch.

"Meghan and Sarah still talked about their road trip, so I pitched another trip, this time with more comfort in a bus and staying in great hotels, stopping at great restaurants and enjoying New Orleans in all its splendor. Meghan and Will are real foodies, so I enticed them with excellent southern cooking.

"That leaves Ryder and Ronny. They're older now and the long, hot ride on a bike isn't their thing anymore. They take their bikes for short spins now. What they like, especially Ronny who works in the wine region, in Temecula, is good food, drinks and great music. Nowadays, they only ride to raceways and watch others twist the throttle. On a long road trip, they don't want to wear leathers any more, but comfy clothes, and they don't want to end up with flies in their teeth. They just want to relax and enjoy.

"I roped in all of you, and here you are.

"Now, enough about me. Confess, one of you. Confess to killing my angel, my sweet. If not I'll kill all of you, one by one. Someone slipped her a deadly drug. When I woke up in the morning, she was lying beside me. She had choked on her own vomit."

"It wasn't us," cried Meghan. "All we did, Sarah and I, was share some rum. We woke up half-way through the night and decided to get the heck out of the cemetery. It was too creepy. Some of you were lying on the ground but we thought you were all sleeping. We walked and walked until we came to an all-night diner. We sobered up with some coffee, took a taxi to the hotel and continued on our way."

"We saw some of you guys spaced out and slumping to the ground. It was so eerie, scary actually. We didn't know what to do so we caught a taxi that was driving by and headed to the hotel and then back home," said Naomi.

"We woke up after the ladies had already gone," said Ryder. "We saw Margie beside you and freaked out. We walked back to the hotel, got our gear and headed back to California."

Turning to Dylan and Jordan, Jonathan said, "That leaves you two, still there, still at the cemetery. You saw Margie. Why didn't you call for an ambulance?"

"We didn't have cell phones in those days. I touched her pulse and she had none. By the time Jordan and I woke up, she was already gone. Sorry. It was horrible, I know. We didn't want to get mixed up with anything. We didn't think you would know who we were or where we came from, so we just high-tailed it out of there," said Dylan. "We were cowards."

"What about you Jonathan, you were out of it. You drank more than half a bottle of Southern Comfort that night. If you would have stayed sober, perhaps your Margie would have survived," said Jordan.

"Are you blaming me for my wife's death now?" he

roared.

"Well, aren't you to blame? Isn't that why you were a hermit in the woods for so many years, because you couldn't face the truth, you killed her and now you're projecting your guilt onto all of us," said Ryder.

"That's not true! No. Never would I kill my love!" Jonathan screamed.

"No one killed your wife," said Dylan.

"What?"

"No one slipped her any drugs that night."

"How do you know that?" asked Jonathan quite perplexed.

"Because after you had finished drinking half a bottle of that liquor, you were in your own private fantasy," said Dylan. "You were fast asleep, sitting on the grass, leaning against a grave stone. Margie confided in me. She said that she loved you very much, but that you two had never really discussed the future. She naturally assumed she would go back to nursing and you took it for granted that she would be a proper minister's wife with all the congregational obligations. She was very uptight. She asked me for a Molly because she had seen me taking one. She wanted to escape her predetermined future life, if only for a little while."

***

Dylan was already tripping in his euphoric fantasy world. Margie popped the pill and waited in anticipation of a passage into another sphere, one of happiness and bliss, but what she got was a front row seat in a theater showing a horror flick within her own mind. Fifteen minutes after swallowing the Molly there was an atomic explosion within her own body. Her heart started racing and the heat generated raised her body temperature to a fever. Her face became flushed and she began to sweat profusely.

Margie looked around and there on a tombstone across the way was a life-size crucifix of Jesus. He was alive, shaking his head and looking at her in judgment and disappointment. But was it really Jesus? No, the face was that of Jonathan who was lecturing her. "A wife must submit to her husband in all things, for he is the head of the wife even as Christ is the head of the church."

"I'm sorry, Jonathan!" she cried.

Jonathan disappeared. She now heard voices, low, throaty voices calling 'Margie, Margie.'

"Who are you? What do you want?" she cried out loud.

Zombie-like figures drifted out of tombs all around her, their clothes tattered, all wearing masks. The stench was unbearable. Margie shrieked. The decaying corpses removed their masks and she instantly recognized them. They were her patients from the nursing home.

"You let us die. You are responsible for our early deaths," they moaned.

"I did everything I could. It's not my fault."

"You should have done more." The walking dead disappeared. Suddenly, right in front of her stood a solitary figure, disfigured and red with two horns protruding from his head.

"I'm here to collect your soul," he said.

"No, no, never. I believe in God."

"But you broke one of his commandments. 'Thou shall not kill.'"

"I have never killed anyone."

"You're killing yourself right now," he laughed. "Suicide is a sin."

"But I didn't mean to. I just wanted a moment of escape from reality," she protested.

"I'm not sorry to tell you that your escape is now permanent."

Margie threw up whatever she had ingested that day, but it didn't all come out. Some of it lodged in her throat. She fell to the ground.

***

"You gave her the drug that killed her," shouted Jonathan.

"I gave it to her because she asked for it," replied Dylan.

"Never! She was pure, virtuous and innocent!"

"She wasn't so innocent," said Mike, standing by the entrance to the tomb. "You put her on a pedestal, but you didn't respect her wishes. She wanted to continue being a nurse and not hidden away in your house or the little church community you were going to lead. Did you listen to her?"

"What are you saying, Mike? You're talking about your little sister."

"I know. And she was sweet and all but you know, as a teenager she wasn't so innocent. She would go to parties and drink too much. A couple of times she stayed over at her girlfriend's house overnight so our parents couldn't see how drunk she was."

"Lies, all lies! Virtuous, modest, pure and chaste, that was Margie."

"You've made her into something she never was. She wasn't bad or anything, just like any other teenager, rebelling against their parents, finding their own way, trying this and trying that. She smoked some reefers with me. She asked me for them."

"Lies! How can you say that. Your own sister!"

"Because it's the truth. Jonathan, these people are probably telling the truth. No one here killed her. No one is a murderer. You have to let them go. You have to own the truth."

"Never! Never! They are all liars, just trying to save their own skins. Dylan murdered her and the rest are accomplices. But I know what to do." Looking at Dylan he said, "If I kill you now you will receive your just punishment but you wouldn't be suffering like I did for all those years. No, it's too quick, too easy. You took away my love, my everything, and now I'm going to do the same to you."

"What are you saying?" asked Dylan.

"I'm going to let you live, but not your wife, Brooke. I think that's fair."

"No," screamed Dylan, "not Brooke, not the mother of my son."

Jonathan had a vile, evil look on his face. He opened the wooden door of the tomb and ran out towards the entrance of the cemetery, on his way to the bus. In that moment, those within the tomb could hear thunder and see lightning in the distance.

"Enough!" said Mike. "I'm not going to be an accessory to murder, especially that of an innocent person." He started up the steps in order to stop Jonathan committing this heinous crime.

"Wait, one second, please untie me," said Ryder, who was closest to Mike, "and I will untie the rest. Mike cut Ryder's ropes. The nine people stumbled out of the tomb.

Their legs were cramped and tingling from too little blood circulation over the last few hours. What met them was a sudden torrential downpour. Lightning could be seen in the near distance, and the time between the strike and the accompanying thunderous crash was only seconds. They could barely see the outline of Jonathan who was running towards the cemetery exit, when suddenly he was hit by a bolt of lightning. They all ran over to where he was lying. Mike was the first to arrive at the horrible scene. Jonathan, lying on his back, had a look of disbelief on his face. He was shaking his head back and forth, and then the look of absolute terror grew in his eyes. He exhaled his last breath and was gone. Mike checked his pulse. There was none.

"You poor, poor fool, Jonathan," he lamented. "For such a long time you had me convinced that one or more of these eight people had murdered my sister. That's why I went along with your insane scheme to force a confession out of them. Look where it's gotten you. What about me. I'll be going to jail for kidnapping. Shit! Why couldn't you just let it be? Gawd!"

Poor Jonathan indeed. Hit by lightning, twice no less. What are the chances? He deceived himself, had misconceptions about the woman he loved. In his eyes, his wife was the perfect woman. But, she really wasn't. She was several levels below perfection. She was normal.

"Mike, do you have a cell phone on you?" asked Sarah who, along with the other seven, had made it to the scene. "We have to call for an ambulance."

"I do," he said half chocking on the words, wallowing in tears, and I will."

"Are our spouses all right?" asked Sarah.

"Yeah, they just got another injection of sleeping fluids

from Jonathan a few hours ago. He didn't want to harm them. They were innocent in his eyes. They'll wake up with a headache in the morning, but they'll be all right.

I'm going to take you all back to the hotel in the bus. You can press charges against me. I don't care. I did help in imprisoning all of you."

"Okay. We'll all wait here until an ambulance and the police arrive. We can't very well leave a body in this cemetery for the second time. That wouldn't be right," said Jordan.

"I don't know about the rest of you, but I won't be pressing any charges against you, Mike. We were cowards back then, and Margie was your sister. I think we should put all this behind us and get on with our lives," said Dylan.

"Mike, you seem to be a decent kind of guy," said Jordan. "How did Jonathan rope you into helping him in his bizarre plan?"

"I'm asking myself the same question right now," replied Mike. "Twenty-five years ago Jonathan came back from New Orleans to Vancouver with my sister's ashes in an urn. Throughout the funeral and everything he didn't speak a single word. He looked as if he were in a trance, or a trauma victim. He left right after that and took up residence in his uncle's cabin in a forested area near a little village in the interior of B.C. I went to see him now and then over the years but he never spoke of my sister or what had happened. After more than a decade he disappeared, along with his old Suburban. Not all that long ago he came to visit me in my apartment. He had changed. He had cut his hair and looked kind of normal. He had been a truck driver for several years driving all over the continent.

"That's when he told me about what had happened to Margie. He said that she had been brutally murdered in New Orleans, that she had been stabbed in the heart. I asked him if the police found the criminal who did this, but he said that the cops had no idea who the perpetrator was since he or she wasn't a local. Back then Jonathan was not able to give the police any information about the people who had been with him in the cemetery. He was in shock and couldn't speak."

"An autopsy must have been done. She obviously wasn't stabbed, she had overdosed, that's why there was no police inquiry," said Dylan.

"Right. But I didn't know that. Jonathan stuck to his story. He was so angry. He told me about the eight people who had accompanied him to the cemetery that evening. It had taken him all these years to remember and find them. Then he told me of his elaborate plan to take them on a Blues tour to New Orleans. There in the cemetery he was going to confront them and find out who the murderer was. He was going to take him or her to the police. That's what he told me. He never said that he wanted to murder any one of the eight people, just bring the guilty person to justice. And, after all these years, I wanted justice for my little sister, so I went along. I mean he had been ordained as a minister all those years ago. I had no idea that he had that much hatred inside of him."

"It destroyed him," said Hannah.

"It did. It almost destroyed me. I couldn't stand looking at you on our trip. That's why I kept my head down most of the time when you were entering the bus."

"Yeah, I would have had a hard time too if that would have happened to one of my loved ones," said Naomi.

"Mike, can you open the doors to the bus? I want to know how Will is, and the others, of course."

"They're still going to be in la-la-land for a few hours. Jonathan gave them quite a strong sedative."

"Nevertheless, once the ambulance arrives I'll ask the attendants to look at all the people on the bus to make sure they're okay," said Meghan.

"I didn't realize that Margie had died," said Sarah, staring into the distance. "I should have helped in some way back then."

"I know what you mean," said Naomi. "We felt uncomfortable and just wanted to get out of there. Much the same feeling I have now, but of course I won't."

"I feel so bad that we left them," said Hannah. "You know, Naomi, we should have listed to that hillbilly, Woody. He told me to turn around and go back home. I still think he must have found a portal into the future."

"You had a warning about not going on, Hannah? So did we, from a spiritual person on an Indian reservation," said Ronny. "How creepy is that?"

"We had a feeling that something wasn't right back then, but it was so dark. We couldn't really see what had happened," said Ryder.

"I was a coward, plain and simple," said Dylan. "I couldn't have done anything for Margie, but I could have tried to find a phone and call for an ambulance, and then gone back to the graveyard so Jonathan didn't have to be alone in there. This haunted me for many years."

Sirens coming closer could be heard in the distance. "Finally, the ambulance and a police car," noted Jordan.

"Let's show Jonathan some respect and tell the police and ambulance attendants who he was," said Meghan.

"And why we are here?" asked Sarah.

"Let's just say that we were on a bus tour and Mike was the driver," said Meghan.

"One other thing," said Ronny. "Ryder and I have gotten to know you guys quite well over the last few days and you're all really great. However, let's make a pact right now."

"A what?" said Jordan in disbelief. "We're not at the Crossroads."

"Well, maybe we are. What I meant to say is, let's make a pact to never ever get together again."

"Amen to that," replied both Naomi and Hannah.

CHAPTER XIV

EPILOGUE

Jonathan is lying dead on the ground in the cemetery. His soul is about to exit his body. The Prince of Darkness suddenly appears. He is there to claim his prize:

Ah, Jonathan!
The moment is now, the moment is here
When I will lead you, into another sphere
The pact that you made, of your own free will
Way back at the Crossroads, you must now fulfill
I'll carry your soul, the essence of you
To my place of torment, my kingdom of woe
I've opened the gates, to the place you will dwell
The fires are lit, in my inferno called hell
Oh wailing you'll hear, and loud piercing screams
By others and you, you'll live your worst dreams

The rain stops quite suddenly. The clouds part and down come the ghost of Margie, accompanied by a host of angels who are singing "Nearer, My God, to Thee." Their tears are falling down upon the corpse of Jonathan, embalming him in a saline solution of sadness.

Margie shouts at the Prince of Darkness:

You monster, you demon, just leave him alone

Go back to your darkness, your fire, brimstone
No sin he committed, no one did he kill
Spent years in a netherworld, his own private hell
He loved me so much, became oh so sad
When I died that night, he truly went mad
The pact that you made you now must withdraw
It's empty and meaningless, by God's holy law
My sweetheart made it with an unsound mind
Rescind your demands, for once be so kind
He once was so helpful, he had empathy
For the sick and the dying and all those in need
I am the one guilty, who caused my love pain
I should be suffering, I am to blame
Scared of my life, that I saw ahead
I turned to drugs, so take me instead
I love him so dearly, I'll go in his place
My sweet will receive God's eternal grace

The Prince of Darkness:
Oh, Margie, Margie!
You want me to believe that:

The eternal feminine will let your soul soar
To far greater heights you've ascended before
But wait, this sounds common, this sounds so blasé
I'm not falling for it, not now, in no way
For this to work, Margie, you'd have to be pure
And virtuous, saintly, you're not, that's for sure
But let me speak freely, and honest as well
Of the things that you fear, be it heaven or hell
Heaven is love, of a mother, a child
And a beautiful sunrise seen outdoors in the wild

Epilogue

And hells on this earth, in war zones, sick minds
Are many and varied, and easy to find
So stop all your cowering to the powers that be
To political tyrants, or devout fantasy
Break free from constraints that are holding you down
And let your minds wander, and then go to town
Be anarchists, rebels, use your own free will
Fight back and be heard, march on, better still
Embrace your own music, be it bebop or blues
The tune in your soul, play upon a kazoo
So, Jonathan and Margie,
Escape all your demons, escape all those beasts
Bring happiness, joy, an eternal feast
Rise far above others, and show them the way
In harmony lead them, strong foundations lay
Music alone, it will set you free
From all earthly boundaries and then you will see
That the God that your fear, and the Devil you dread
They do not exist, they're just in your head!

As he speaks his last word, the Prince of Darkness dissolves into nothingness. The choir of angels vaporizes into a fluffy cumulus cloud. Jonathan and Margie are re-embodied beside the tombstone where Margie passed away all those years ago. Another person is suddenly standing beside them. It is Robert Johnson. They look at one another in bewilderment.

Margie:	*So what do we do now?*
Jonathan:	*What He said.*
Robert:	*We live the BLUES.*

ACKNOWLEDGEMENTS

I would like to thank my daughter Marnie Klose-Dibisch and my very good friend Christian Hänggi for being so supportive of my writing over many, many years. Their insights, suggestions and ideas have always been very important to me. They have, as in the books I have written before, been very helpful in improving and polishing my manuscript and thereby transforming it into a cogent and coherent book.

A big thank you to Amber Gulbis, who coordinated a competition for creativity in illustration where I was able to pick the amazing image of the front cover. Amber was instrumental in a similar process for my book Confess or Die.

Thank you also to Anastasia Salikhova who created the beautiful front cover illustration and to Deann Ford who turned the illustration into a wonderful book cover.

Thank you very much also to my granddaughter Isabella who just became a teenager. She has a passion for writing. I asked her to write a chapter for me, that of Hannah and Naomi. She did. Well, I didn't really use any of it in my book, but what I did get out of her writing was the strong and determined personalities of those two young women and this helped me tremendously in developing those characters. Keep writing, Izzy.

THE AUTHOR

Heidi Klose was born in Germany. At the age of nine she emigrated to the Niagara Region in Canada with her mother, joining her two older brothers who had already settled there. Heidi began writing song lyrics and poems as a teenager and has enjoyed writing ever since. She is a graduate of Brock University with a degree in History and German. She is the mother of three adult children and grandmother to four adorable children. She has written several children's books and two adventure novels, *A French River Adventure* and *The French River Delta – The Legend of Makadewaa.* Her passion for reading murder mysteries and historical novels influenced the creation of *Darkness Falls on Niagara,* a historical fiction in which three youngsters solve a 200-year-old mystery. It is the prequel to the book *Fine Dining in Niagara – To Die For. Confess or Die* is her tribute to Agatha Christie, her favorite murder mystery writer. *Backroad Blues*, is Heidi's latest book. It was inspired by her daughter's travels through the United States in a Westfalia camper and by two legends of sinister origin. Heidi lives in St. Catharines, Ontario, with her husband Martin.